ANGEL WING MINISTRIES PRESENTS

...

FORGIVING FREEDOM

CARRIED BY ANGELS SERIES

BOOK NUMBER 3

Brenda Conley
Angel Wing Ministries

COVER DESIGN
CREATED
BY

BRANDON ANDRINA

Library of Congress Cataloging in-Publication Data
Conley, Brenda
Forgiving Freedom/Brenda Conley
ISBN-13: 978-0692259962 (Angel Wing Ministries)
ISBN-10: 0692259961

DEDICATION

This book belongs to all the broken women who live everyday with the grief of losing a child to the lies of abortion.

God sees your brokenness. He wants to restore you. Our God is in the restoration business and He loves you.

Do not let satan tell you differently. He wants you to live a lifetime of brokenness. He is a liar who comes to kill, steal and destroy. He will never have a victory unless you give it to him. He has already been defeated. Jesus himself went into hell and took back the keys so that satan could have no control over any area of your life.

There is no sin that is too big for our God to forgive. He does not want you to live a life carrying a load of regret. He made a way through His Son Jesus Christ to lighten that load and give you hope. In fact, He will pick you up and carry you when the road seems too long… when you are too weary…when you have gone as far as you can…when you can see no hope at the end of the day.

If you are still burdened with choices that you made, today is the day to lay them at the feet of Jesus. He is just waiting for you to come just as you are. Broken and spilled out, surrendered to Him. Feel the freedom that only He can give. Run to His mercy seat and live with joy. Jesus is just waiting to change your life. He wants to give you a life everlasting full of love, hope and peace; the peace that surpasses all understanding.

By ourselves we will never be worthy. But through Christ all things are possible. He loves you enough that He laid down His life for you so you could live a life abundant. You were created with a purpose. God knew that purpose even before you were brought into this world. Seek Him. Find Him. Live for Him.

ACKNOWLEDGMENTS

Praise God from whom all blessings flow. Without Him, I could not do any of this. It was His idea, His message and His provision that allowed me to write these words. He is my Lord and Savior, The Keeper of my heart, My Provider, My Deliverer, My One and Only, My All in All. I love You Lord. Use me as a vessel to carry your story around the world.

Thank you to all of the brave women who were willing to share their experiences with me. Without all of you these books would not have been written. I am so proud of each one of you. Because of you, God allowed me to write His message of hope. God began to drop each of you into my life and you opened your hearts and shared your pain and suffering. If through these words, one woman makes the decision to choose life for her baby, then heaven will rejoice. God bless all of you as you walk towards a forgiving Father whose arms stretch out wide. My prayer is that God will use these books to reach multitudes of people who believe there is only one way. I pray these books will be a vessel for the broken that cannot see past their sorrow, a way to conquer the fear that they may find themselves living with everyday. Let God have His way in your life. Feel His love. My hope is to strengthen young women before…

As my family continues to grow, I am constantly reminded of the responsibility we as parents will always have. When our children are babies we are consumed with teaching them how to walk and talk. Through the school years we are guiding and directing. As young adults, we are preparing to release them into a world. The preparation has been a life long task. Hopefully by this step, they know their Lord and Savior and they are ready to embrace God's purpose for them. As of this writing, Ron and I have 4 children, 3 daughters-in-law, 1 son-in law, 7 grandsons,

2 granddaughters and another baby on the way. Our job, though changing, continues to multiply yearly.

I want to say thank you to my husband of 40 years. Ron, as childhood sweethearts, we have grown up together. We have birthed our babies, raised amazing adults and ushered loved ones into the presence of the Lord. We have walked into the unknown fearlessly one day at a time. Looking back now, I stand in amazement at how the years have flown by. Only with you Baby. May God bless us daily. I can't wait to see where He is going to take us as we learn more about Him everyday.

I have two prayer partners, their names may seem familiar when I tell you. Genie Garcia and Debbie Smith have helped me to grow in the Lord. They have blessed me. They bring love, teaching, chastisement when necessary, and a joy to find our Savior. Genie has taught me to stand; Debbie has increased my love walk. Thank you girls for all you have been to me. Our love transcends time and space.

Thank you to all who have read my books and found blessings. May the seeds that have been planted continue to grow and may your lives be changed forever.

Again...To all of you...God is why I write. Without His lead, there would be no words. It is my pleasure to bring you His messages of hope. Don't take my word though. Pick up a Bible. Find a lifetime full of love and wisdom. See how much He really loves you. Nothing can compare to the real deal. He is waiting for you in the pages of His word. He has a special message, created just for you that only He can deliver. He is that personal. Let Him love you.

TO GOD BE THE GLORY, GREAT THINGS HE HAS DONE

All My Love,
Mom

STORY CHARACTERS

Naming the characters in my stories is like giving birth to my own children. I have always thought it important that they have strong names that will serve them well through life. I decided it was important that I share with you why I chose the names of the people that you would meet in this story.

Noelle--(French origin meaning "born at Christmas time) she is a broken 19 year old. The oldest daughter in what was supposed to be a wonderful family. If asked, they would tell you that they are Christians; however, Christmas, Easter and marriages sum up their church life experience as a family. Noelle and her sisters attended summer Vacation Bible School programs and you will see how the Word of God is faithful. You will walk with her through a life changing experience. See how God made a way for her through all of it. All she had to do was look at His hand guiding and directing her path.

Brad Conroy--(English origin meaning "one who has broad shoulders") a hard working 22 year old whose life is about to change as he follows his heart into an area of God's leading. Brad is faithful to wait upon the Lord and wise enough to honor his father and mother. See the turn his life takes, as he is obedient to the Lord.

Eyan Conroy--(Gaelic origin; form of John meaning "God is gracious") Brad's brother. They are different and yet so close. He loves and respects his brother. At 20 years old, he is ready to embrace the world. Eyan is looking to branch out into the world of the unknown. Living on the farm is not in his future. His passion is to reach the lost for the Lord out on a mission field somewhere adventurous.

Angelina Conroy--(Greek form of Angela, meaning "a heavenly messenger; an angel") her name really represents the part that she will play in Noelle's life. Angelina is a

survivor; full of wisdom and willing to walk through the ugliness of her past life to help save the life of an unborn child.
Terran Conroy--(Latin origin; Man of the earth) Angelina's husband, Brad, and Eyan's father. A wonderful man who left this earth too soon. They miss him desperately. He lives on in the character of the boys as they grow into the men he would have wanted them to be.
Genie Smith--(English origin; form of Jean meaning, "God is gracious") Noelle's mother. Trying to heal from a broken marriage, her focus becomes her girls.
Gale Smith--(Irish origin meaning a foreigner) this was the husband to Genie and father to their daughters. His leaving caused a hole in their family that left them trying to figure out who they are. He really did become a foreigner to them.
Aunt Debbie--(Hebrew origin; in the Bible a prophetess) Genie's sister. She loves her sister and nieces and wants only to help support them.
Nissa--(Hebrew origin; meaning "one who tests others") the middle sister. Thrust into becoming the protector in the home. She loves her sisters desperately and is the peacemaker in the family. Seventeen years old and starting her senior year of high school.
Anaya--(African origin; meaning "One who looks up to God) the youngest of the three girls. Anaya and Noelle have the closest bond of the girls. She feels Noelle's pain the most. She is going to be sixteen.
Michael Dunn--(Hebrew origin; meaning, "Who is like God") Genie's boss. His life is touched by watching this family walk through fire and come out on the other side with a deeper relationship with the Lord.
Michelle Jordan--(French origin and feminine form of Michael meaning, "Who is like God") She, apart from anyone else, will be able to come along side Noelle. They become friends through an understanding of brokenness.

Shawn Murray--(Irish origin and a form of John, meaning, "God is gracious") Shawn is laughter when times get hard. There is always a smile waiting from him. He is one of the broken that God dropped into the Conroy's lives. His early years were full of sorrow and sadness.

Pastor Travis Gates--(French meaning, "To cross over") Brad's youth pastor. He has been a grounding point for the Conroy boys while they were growing up. He will be helpful in showing Noelle the way towards healing through Christ.

Rebecca Gates—(Hebrew meaning, "One who is bound to God") she is Pastor Travis' wife and they exhibit a love joined through Christ. She brings completeness to Travis.

Delmyn Whitehall--(English origin meaning a man of the mountain) this is a troubled young man. His life was full of money and no responsibility. There has been no accountability until his world comes crashing down around him. This man will represent an amazing opportunity to practice forgiveness.

Tempo (Teo for short) Leroy Mohan--(Spanish for "a godly man") An attorney who's path will cross Delmyn's and will have an impact on this young man's life.

Pastor Preston Cronkhite--(English meaning, "from the priest's town") The pastor who would be the first to connect with Delmyn during his incarceration. His heart is for the lost and broken.

Professor Lee and Patty--(English meaning, "from the meadow". English meaning, "feminine form of Patrick; of noble descent") See how God masterminds their path crossing Genie and the girls's.

Come along with me as we follow our friends through this new adventure. Be prepared for the turns that this story will take. They even surprised me. Noelle has so many decisions to make. She has so much to learn. However, praise God that she has put her life in greater hands…The Hands of God…who holds every tear that we cry.

Chapter One

Psalm 32:1

Blessed is he

whose transgressions

are forgiven,

whose sins are covered.

PSALM 32

1. *Blessed is he whose transgressions are forgiven, whose sins are covered.*

2. *Blessed is the man whose sin the LORD does not count against him and in whose spirit is no deceit.*

3. *When I kept silent, my bones wasted away through my groaning all day long.*

4. *For day and night your hand was heavy upon me; my strength was sapped as in the heat of summer.*
Selah

5. *Then I acknowledged my sin to you and did not cover up my iniquity. I said, "I will confess my transgressions to the LORD" and you forgave the guilt of my sin.*
Selah

6. *Therefore let everyone who is godly pray to you while you may be found; surely when the mighty waters rise, they will not reach him.*

7. *You are my hiding place; you will protect me from trouble and surround me with songs of deliverance.*
Selah

8. *I will instruct you and teach you in the way you should go; I will counsel you and watch over you.*

9. *Do not be like the horse or the mule, which have no understanding but must be controlled by bit and bridle or they will not come to you.*

10. *Many are the woes of the wicked, but the LORD'S unfailing love surrounds the man who trusts in him.*

11. *Rejoice in the LORD and be glad, you righteous; sing, all you who are upright in heart!*

say. It matters what you do. See, Noelle's problem didn't start with the rape. It started with the hurt created by her father and the inability of Noelle to forgive. Unforgivingness never wins. It is self-destructive. Jesus gave us the gift of forgiveness from the cross. From that moment on, we had the option to live free or caught in the bondage of unforgivingness. The choice was freely given to each of us.

Will Noelle be able to work her way through the forgiveness she needs to offer her father and the man that raped her? Will she find healing?

Come along with us as we continue on the journey in FORGIVING FREEDOM.

Mark 11:25
And when you stand praying, if you hold anything against anyone, forgive him, so that your Father in heaven may forgive you your sins.

I PETER 1:18-21

For you know that it was not with perishable things such as silver and gold that you were redeemed from the empty way of life handed down to you from your fore-fathers,

but with the precious blood of Christ, a lamb without blemish or defect.

He was chosen before the creation of the world, but was revealed in these last times for your sake.

Through Him you believe in God, who raised Him from the dead and glorified Him, and so your faith and hope are in God.

Get this...You are a chosen people, a royal priesthood. You belong to God. But...Know this...He isn't a dictator. He won't force you to come to Him. He will lovingly call you, waiting patiently for you to open the door to your heart and welcome Him in.

Noelle found the love of the Lord. She has accepted the ugly thing that has happened to her and she is learning to rejoice in the coming baby that is the fruition of the rape. God, in all His wisdom, was already master minding a plan for her life that would bring her into the desires of her heart. You see, the bad choices she made after her father left her family, brought her into a place that allowed satan to attack her life. She opened the door. He grabbed an opportunity to reek havoc in another life.

Through the blood of the cross, Noelle was able to close that door and push satan back. We have to overcome evil with good. It doesn't matter what you

INTRODUCTION

> We owed a debt we couldn't pay.
> Jesus paid a debt He didn't owe.

We have reached the third book in this series, CARRIED BY ANGELS. In the first book, SAVING NOELLE, we watched as, on the run, scared and desperate, Noelle found the love of a Savior that gave her hope and a future. We watched as she experienced the love of others who knew and were willing to share His love. Her life changed and so did the lives of her mother and sisters. God was able to help them find their way through brokenness and sorrow. He was able to put their life back together. His plan was above anything she could have imagined.

In book two, PERFECT LOVE, we rejoice as Noelle's life is united with the man God created especially for her. The book ends with Brad and Noelle binding their love and beginning to build a new life together. God became the center of their relationship. They allowed Him to have His way and we can only anticipate the adventure God will take them through.

Book three, FORGIVING FREEDOM, will give us an opportunity to embrace the act of forgiveness. Remember this...There is forgiveness for every person no matter what they have done. A price has been paid for you and me. That price wasn't cheap. In fact it was unbelievably costly. The sacrifice was given by God, His only son, Jesus. We were purchased with the blood of Jesus. He shed it willingly for each and everyone of us. Listen to this.

FOREWORD

These are the words of one of the most amazing women I have the pleasure to know. She shared this with me one day and I was impressed to share them with you. May they bless you as they have blessed me.

****

I am trying to wrap my head and my heart around the great love God has for me. You see I still have such a long way to go. I am so not worthy of that kind of love and I am at once relieved that He loves me anyway and confused that I am still continually admonished due to my sin nature.

How? How do I stop sinning? I certainly have been able to experience deliverance from many things. Still...Some open doors won't shut and old habits hang on. So what do I do with these stubborn stains? One day I feel washed clean only to find the reappearing stain of sin glaring at me off what should be a pristine wedding gown.

I should be dressed and waiting to meet my groom; but instead I scrub furiously at one stain after another.

It seems to be an unending job and I am sad. But then I hear from someone else that my groom does not see my stains and I long to see myself through His eyes; so that I would know for sure that He sees me as lovely and worthy to be His bride.

Debbie Smith.
December 29, 2008

JUDGE OWEN MARSHALL WAS STARRING DEEPLY INTO the eyes of, what he would classify as, 'the little rich boy' standing in front of him. "Young man, this is a horrendous crime you've been accused of committing. I don't feel like you are taking seriously the direction your life just turned."

"Oh no sir...I understand fully what's happening here today. But...I didn't do it. Do you understand? I'm pleading not guilty." Delmyn Whitehall stood before the Judge in his three-piece suit, immaculate starched white shirt and classic tie. He stood with arrogance and pride wearing a smug look of someone who had it all together. He was confident and sure. Del knew his dad was going to get all of this worked out. By the end of this arraignment, this nightmare was going to be nothing but a technicality. Any minute now, he would be free again and that would be none too soon. He'd had enough of all of the noise in infernal jail. Yesterday they had brought some riffraff into the cell and the person was just stupid. A whole day listening to him yelling about knowing his rights and wanting to talk to his lawyer had been enough for Del. The guy was strung out on something crazy and he didn't even know his name let alone his rights. Oh yeah! He was ready to get out of this mess right now.

Del stood dressed in his finest. His shirt starched as stiffly as his attorney's. In any other situation, it would have been difficult to differentiate between their roles. However, they were not in any other situation and the judge was not impressed with Delmyn's demeanor, regardless of the picture he portrayed. In fact, Judge Marshall, due to his background, was completely

1

annoyed with Mr. Whitehall's lack of respect.

Owen Marshall came out of poverty. His father died when he was four and he was raised by a hard working mother who told him he could be anything he wanted to be. He worked hard in school and received many scholarships so he could continue his education. It was by working long hours at jobs he hated and going to school full time that brought him to this point in life. He had zero tolerance for adults who had been born with a silver spoon in their mouth and did nothing with the blessings they had been given.

The young man standing in front of him represented his idea of the "lazy, spoiled, rich kid".

"Mr. Whitehall I understand more than you think. I understand you are an obnoxious, arrogant punk who doesn't have enough sense to show respect to the person of authority who will be a part of making decisions that affect your life forever." Judge Marshall continued, "Furthermore, you have an attorney representing you and I am silencing you. From this moment on, I will only hear from Mr. Mohan. Is that clear Mr. Mohan? Otherwise your client will be in contempt of court."

"Yes sir Your Honor." Teo Mohan respectfully answered while he grabbed a hold of his client's suit jacket and gave it a quick jerk. He hoped Delmyn got the message to shut his mouth.

"Hey wait a minute. I pay for this attorney and I'll say when he talks or when he doesn't." Del opened his mouth again.

Mohan thought, *obviously he didn't understand my tug.* "Your Honor...if I may have a moment with my client?"

Banging his gavel, Judge Marshall decreed, "That will be $100.00 fine with another night served in

2

the jail for Mr. Delmyn Whitehall. Bailiff, remove this man from **MY** courtroom."

Teo understood the emphasis on "**MY**" even if Whitehall didn't.

Del began to scream, "You can't do that. I'm not going to stay another night." Turning to face his dad, Del pleaded, "Dad? Do something. He can't talk to me like I'm a nobody. I'm not going back there. I can't."

The Bailiff was already ushering him out of the courtroom.

"Son, stop arguing. You're only making the situation worse." Del's dad, Keefe Whitehall, pleaded with his son as he was physically removed from the room. His heart was breaking. He did not understand how any of this could have happened. His son was a good boy. He could never do any of the terrible things those girls were saying. He understood boys would be boys. He also understood that some girls put themselves in situations that bring them trouble. The world was full of good girls and then there were...You know...The bad girls. What is Del to do when the bad girls throw themselves at him? After all, he is only human. His body anatomy responds differently. It is not his fault. Right? Besides what was he going to tell Shauna, Del's mother? She was back at their home waiting for her son to come back to the house with his dad. This was not going at all the way he had hoped it would. What good was the attorney he had hired? After paying out all of that money, you would think things should have gone differently.

"Dad...do something. I can't go back there." Del was yelling over his shoulder as the Bailiff closed the door.

"Mr. Mohan, we will reconvene tomorrow at

3

this same time. I hope by then your client will have had enough time to take the good advice I am sure you are going to offer him."

"Yes sir, Your Honor. I hope so too. Thank you."

Receiving a nod from the judge the courtroom clerk announced, "Next case. Anderson vs. the State of Georgia."

"What?" Keefe looked at the attorney who was walking towards him. "What happened?" He asked.

Taking the arm of the father, Teo Mohan said, "Let's talk outside." He walked him straight out of the courtroom doors and to a nearby bench in a private alcove.

"Mr. Whitehall, what happened in there was one of the worst displays of immaturity I have ever witnessed. Your son must learn to keep his mouth shut. No judge is going to allow disrespect for his authority in his courtroom. On top of that, the felony they have charged him with is a crime of total disrespect for another human life. We are going to have a hard time convincing a jury that your son respects others when the show that he puts on bears resemblance to the total opposite. Now I suggest if he calls you, it would be to his advantage for you to convince him that tomorrow when he appears before Judge Marshall again, he resembles a changed man. I expect his demeanor would be apologetic and humble." Teo said.

"Humble?" Keefe questioned.

"Yes sir...Humble. It is not a sign of weakness. It's a good character for any man to exhibit." Teo ended with a look on his face that said he was finished.

"Well maybe he needs a different attorney, if that's the best advice you can give?" Keefe Whitehall rose up to his almost six-foot height.

4

Taking a deep breath Tempo Leroy Mohan said in a definite voice, "That **IS** the best advice I or any other attorney could give. Nevertheless, if you think that is not good enough for you and your son, then fine. If that is what you want, go for it. I promise you my heart will not break if I do not have to deal with your son's ill temper. He's the most arrogant, irresponsible young man I've had the uncanny luck to meet in a long time." With that, Teo Mohan turned to leave.

Keefe, realizing what it would look like if his son walked back into the courtroom tomorrow with a different attorney said, "Wait...Let's not get hasty. After all, you have already spoken with my son. I think we should continue as is...For the time being anyway. Do not get me wrong. I do understand my son can be a bit, shall we say 'anxious' from time to time. Will you be seeing him before tomorrow?" He politely asked.

"It would not be my first choice. However, I will make it a point to see him and give him instruction before we enter that courtroom again. I may have been lax in assuming he would have understood the importance of showing the judge respect." Teo hoped he had driven home his point that respect is something Del should have learned at an early age from his parents.

"I would appreciate any help you could give him. His mother is going to be so disappointed that he is still in jail. I'm not sure what I'm going to tell her."

"I suggest you tell her the truth. Say that her son was belligerent to the judge and he got his hands slapped. Let her know it is not going to go well for him if he doesn't learn some respect before we get into this. Maybe if he calls her, she could talk some sense into him. With that, Teo turned to leave. Having second thoughts he turned back saying, "Mr. Whitehall, just so you can prepare your wife, this isn't going to be pretty. I have seen the girls' statements. The press is going to grab a hold of this. A story like this sells papers. You will find your son on all of the local TV and radio news shows. There will be reporters digging into every aspect of Delmyn's life. Probably you and your wife will be dragged through the eye of the needle also. Be ready. Your life is about to be turned upside down. I suggest you let your son know that. We are in for a fight. It does not sound to me like these girls are going to back down. In fact there are more girls speaking up by the hour." Tipping his head to the broken father, he turned and walked away.

Standing in the hall all alone, Keefe questioned silently to a son who wasn't even there, *Del, what have you gotten us into this time?*

****

Teo Mohan was so angry when he left the court house he could hardly see the steps in front of him as he angrily marched down. He turned right, walking away from his office which was just a block down the street to the left. Not even thinking about where he was going, he walked with a determination. He was headed to walk the "ugly" off; trying to rid himself of the situation that often felt as if it were all encompassing.

Too many times lately he was angry. That wasn't even a good word for how he was feeling. Where do these punks come from? What was fed into their lives that allowed them to get to this point and end up looking like Delmyn Whitehall.

"I don't understand Lord", he spewed out loud. "What makes them think they have the right to treat people the way they do? How can I continue to defend people like him? This is getting too hard."

You love them because I first loved them. Just as I first loved you.

Teo knew the answer before he even asked the question. But what if he couldn't do it any more. *Lord are you going to understand if I can't? What if I can't do it?* His heart broke knowing the answer he was going to hear.

You can do all things through me. I strengthen you.

Father, I know. I know. But sometimes I just want to do something different. Something that doesn't have anything to do with people who do stupid things.

I called you to this through the gospel, that you might share in the glory of the Lord Jesus Christ. So then stand and hold to the teachings.

Teo knew where this was coming from. He had been handed this passage from the Lord a long time ago. 2 Thessalonians 2:14-15 and then the prayer that he repeated so may times.

May our Lord Jesus Christ himself and God our Father, who loved us and by His grace, gave us eternal encouragement and good hope, encourage your hearts and strengthen you in every good deed and word. AMEN.

Over and over he repeated it until it began to calm his spirit. This was the place where God had put him. This time in his life was a service to the Lord. Whether he wanted to do this or not...He would. This was his season in time until the Lord moved him in a different direction.

Okay Lord. I get it. I am here to stay for right now. You will have to stay right by my side. Please don't leave me here alone. I am feeling tired.

Taking deep breaths, he finished the walk that took him down the hill, around and through a peaceful section of town and then to the water's edge. His pace slowed as he walked the board walk following the meandering glide of the river. The slow dance of the water soothed his nerves and allowed him those moments he needed to renew. His thoughts went to one of his favorite scriptures that seemed to sum up his needs:

> ***As the deer pants for streams of water,***
> ***So my soul pants for you, O God***
> ***Psalm 42:1***

This walk was becoming more and more necessary. For ten years he had been doing his job. He represented those who did wrong. He fought for their rights. Along the way there had been those whom he had been able to show the God who loved them. But more than not, they ignored him. Laughing, rebuking or ridiculing. As he thought on the years and the people, the anger in him began to surface again.

My son, there is a time to sow and a time to reap. There will be those that plant and there will be those who harvest. Your job is to spread my Word so that it may be honored.

But Father, I haven't seen any success in so long. I see them set free and then they're back again in trouble. They aren't understanding. Maybe I'm not the right one for this job. Maybe You have a better servant who would have more success for You. Teo continued to argue with the Lord. *I'm becoming weary.*

You will be delivered from the wicked and evil men. For not everyone has faith. But the LORD is faithful, and He will strengthen and protect you from the evil one.

8

Show them love my son. Show them who I am. Before the beginning of time I called you. Show them love.

Okay, Father, I'll show them. But don't You leave me. I need You. You're my Rock and my Refuge. In You I will put my trust.

I am here my son. For eternity. I will never depart from you.

Teo finished his river walk and climbed the hill. Turning left it was only a few feet before he was walking up onto the porch that opened up into his office. It was a small house that had been his working spot for most of the years he had been in practice. A close location to the jail and the court house, it afforded him the space he needed to be accessible when those who had gotten themselves in trouble needed help.

Delmyn Whitehall's father had walked into this office the day before, after hearing his son had been arrested for rape. Now, one day later, there were more girls coming forward and the message was always the same. Parties, drugs, date rape.

Not all of the girls had gone to the hospital. In fact so far it looked like only these last two had gone. But the rape kit wasn't going to help set Mr. Whitehall free. As far as Teo could tell, there wasn't a DNA test done yet. That was just a matter of time now though. A newly passed law now permitted the state to swab for DNA all those who are incarcerated. Soon, they'll come looking to swab. Teo planned to hold that off as long as he could, after all a man was innocent until proven guilty.

****

Back in a cell, Del was boiling mad. Pacing his cell he raged through his conversation, "Who did that judge think he was dealing with anyway? I'll show him he can't talk to a Whitehall like that. Why...I'll bet my dad will be reminding him how much money it takes to run a reelection campaign. I need to talk to Dad." Grabbing a hold of the cell bars in frustration he yelled, "Hey, what do I have to do to make a phone call?" Del continued, "Listen...I need to call someone and I need to talk to my attorney." No one seemed to care. "Do you know who I am?" He yelled again and again.

Somewhere from down the long cell hall a voice yelled back, "Heck no! They don't care who you are... And neither do we. Shut up!"

Del was fuming mad. *When I get out of here I'm going to start a citizen's activist group to change the conditions in this jail. It's criminal the way the police treat people who are locked up. After all, I'm innocent until proven guilty. Isn't that right?* Again he yelled out to whoever was listening, "Hey...I'm Del Whitehall and I want to make a phone call."

****

"What do you mean my son is back in jail? How is that even possible?" Shauna Whitehall was ashen as she voiced her disapproval.

"Well it's possible because Del was disrespectful to the judge." Keefe sternly told his wife.

"I'm sure he's worried about what's happening. You know how he gets when things aren't going his way."

"Listen to me Shauna," Keefe was trying to be as gentle as he possibly could with the mother of his son; yet he wanted her to know and understand the severity of the situation they were facing. "Del is in big trouble Honey and this is going to make a huge mess of our lives. His attorney tells me there are multiple girls coming forward making the same accusations about things he's done to them. I don't know exactly what they're saying; I just know it isn't good. The last thing he needs to do is make the judge angry with him. Do you understand what I'm saying?"

"What I understand is he needs a different attorney. How can someone represent him who thinks he may not be able to win the case. I don't believe for one minute..." Shauna began to cry.

"It doesn't matter what you believe. It matters what the Jury will believe. He needs to paint a picture that looks better than he painted today; one that will sway the jury over to his side. All charm. That's what we're going to tell him if he calls. Right?"

"Okay." She answered unsure if she was strong enough to watch her only son be accused of sins he could not have possibly committed.

"He's a good boy Keefe...a good boy."

"No Shauna...He's a man. And now he has to act like a man."

Keefe kissed the forehead of his beautiful wife. He couldn't help but think about how blessed their life had been. As an investor, his father had been very successful. After his passing the company had been willed to Keefe, the only son. Someday he would pass it on to his only son. Their fortune would be considered old money. The company had continued to make good investments and a wealth had accumulated that was more than they could ever spend in a lifetime.

However, Delmyn had given it quite a go already.

11

As parents they hadn't been able to say no to the boy that had wrapped them around his little finger. He always drove the best cars and took friends on expensive vacations. He was never short of purchases to be made. Every month Keefe was amazed at the amount of money a his son could spend.

Maybe they should have been stricter. Perhaps they should have made more rules for him to follow. He was the only high school student that had his own house. It was in the back of their estate with the pool separating the two houses. Del had always thought he needed his own space. There probably were too many nights of parties that weren't appropriate for someone his age. As his parents, we always thought it was better to have the parties here where we could watch the comings and goings. After all, no parent wants to get that call in the middle of the night saying their child has been in an accident. This way he was home and there was plenty of room for his friends to stay without driving anywhere. Yes, we knew they were drinking. But, at least they weren't doing drugs. Del promised they were clean parties. He never gave us any reason not to believe him. Now was no time to start thinking differently. He was going to support his son. That's what a father does.

Keefe's father had handled family his own way; always working, never having time to spend with a small son. From the very beginning Keefe knew the life he had with his son would look different. He would be there. They would do things together. And they had. But it always seemed that Del dictated what they did and how they did it. Keefe didn't mind. He was just happy to be a part of his son's life. It could be worse. Right?

Enough second guessing the past. They were living in the now. And the now wasn't looking so good.

Tomorrow would have to be a better day. Somehow this nightmare had to go away. Keefe Whitehall wasn't sure how to make that happen; but somehow he would have to try.

Being honest with himself, there had been other times when Del had gotten into something questionable. Up until now though, Keefe could always step in and fix it. Sometimes it just needed a little money thrown in the right direction or a conversation with the right person. A few promises here and a donation or two there. It's amazing how easily people will surrender when you find out their weak spot. Always he had been able to make everything go away without Shauna finding out about it. A follow up conversation with Del always translated into, "Sorry Dad. You know how things get with guys. I'll be more careful next time."

Now it seemed like there wasn't anything for him to do...And that just wasn't acceptable. Keefe was good at finding the soft spot of people; so that's what he decided he would. He would do some checking and find out all he could about Judge Marshall. For goodness sakes, all of this money had to be good for something. It certainly should buy the best legal representation. He could hire a private investigator to do some digging. Let's see what a little digging could come up with. Plus, he would have the investigator find out all he could about this Teo Mohan. Maybe he wasn't the best guy for the job. Or maybe he was. That was yet to be seen. At least when he talked with Del he could tell him he was on top of it. He could give his son something to hang on to. Let him know his dad was on his side.

✸✸✸✸✸✸✸✸✸✸✸✸✸✸✸

Del had quieted down. He realized all of the yelling in the world wasn't going to make them do what he wanted. It was becoming clear to him that no one in this jail cared who he was or even who his dad was. He had never been in a situation like this before. Panic began to rise. He could feel the burning gases rushing into his throat. He was going to throw up. In the corner of the cell was a toilet. The thought of touching that nasty thing wasn't enough to stop his stomach from emptying.

Barely making it to the corner, the burning continued as he gagged and gagged. There really wasn't anything in his stomach. He couldn't even remember when he'd eaten last. There had been trays of food brought to him; but they didn't look very appealing and he really wasn't hungry. Now the acid that was eating at his insides was worse than if there had been food to bring up.

Finishing, he splashed water on his face from the little sink attached to the wall beside the toilet. Sitting back onto the bed, the weight of his situation began to sink in. Without any warning, he was sobbing; uncontrollable, gut wrenching sobs that would not stop.

"How did this happen to me?" He asked out loud. "I don't understand. This kind of stuff doesn't happen to a Whitehall."

Del's mind went back to junior high school. He was in the day, as if he was back there again in the very expensive, elite private school paid for by his father's money. The sun was shining and the manicured grass was a deep green. The breeze was blowing gently across the campus. There were kids everywhere sitting, standing, laughing, walking, and talking. He'd been bugging this goofy kid from his math class. Looking back now, he

14

wasn't even sure why he was doing it.

He had just shoved him down to the ground. The guys that hung around with Del were in a circle so no one could see what Del was doing. They were all laughing and poking fun at the kid on the ground with glasses. Joey. That was his name. Joey McKenzie. He was a free tuition student from an area into which no one from Del's family would never venture. He was just a poor student, a transplant that a local church was giving an opportunity of a lifetime. Del wasn't sure why these wandering thoughts were making him feel uncomfortable.

"Stay down. Don't you get up." Shoving Joey again Del yelled, "I said stay down."

Joey just looked at him. He didn't say anything and he didn't move again. He didn't even look scared. He just looked. He didn't take his eyes off of the guy standing over him and yelling.

Del remembered that Joey's staring made him angry. To this day he knew how much he didn't like it that Joey wasn't yelling back or trying to get up.

"Whatever!" Del said, as he gave him a hard kick right into his ribs.

Joey flinched; but he still just laid there. He didn't even grab his side. He just kept looking straight into the eyes of his attacker.

Del turned to walk away with all of his cronies following him. But he turned back. He remembered looking at Joey and there was Joey still looking at him; still not moving, still not yelling.

He wasn't sure why he'd thought about Joey. He hadn't given him a thought in all of these years. But for some reason he could still remember the look on his face as he walked away. Del hated that Joey didn't fight back.

15

He just laid there on the ground with everyone laughing at him. There was no expression on his face as he looked directly into Del's eyes.

Sitting on the hard bed, in the stink and noise; considering where he was, he wondered why he did what he did? The questions hit him like a brick. *What kind of an animal am I? Why would I find pleasure in doing that to someone else? What is the matter with me?*

Chapter Two

Psalm 32:2

Blessed is the man

whose sin the LORD

does not count against him

and in whose spirit

is no deceit.

NOELLE WOKE UP NEXT TO THE MAN WHO WAS now her husband. She lay very quiet so she could study him while he slept. His dark brown hair had that early morning ruffle. It looked as if someone had run their fingers through the silky waves and didn't smooth it down. His breathing was even and calm. He didn't appear to have a care in the world. His lips were in a soft smile. Was he happy? The answer seemed to be yes.

Those lips. Those were the lips that had kissed her so sweetly last night. Gently loving her as if she were a precious jewel. She had never felt more treasured. How could she be this lucky. After all that had happened to her; the rape, getting pregnant, running away, considering an abortion; look how God had protected her and brought her right into the loving arms of the most wonderful family she could have found.

I'll never stop thanking Him for all He has done in my life. On my own I would have messed things up so badly. She was praising God for Brad and Angelina; her new family. Her husband and now mother-in-law. What if Angelina hadn't been willing to share her past with her. Where would she be now. What about the life of her unborn child. Could she have gone ahead with the abortion? Could she have taken this baby's life? Would she have believed the lies they tell you at the clinics? It's just a mass of cells. Viable life doesn't start until the undeveloped fetus can survive outside of the womb. Easier on your body to have an early abortion than it is to carry a baby full term. All lies. Now she had time to think without the pressure that had weighed her down.

Now she could put her fear in perspective.

Noelle pressed her hand to her stomach; it was showing the bulge indicating her baby was growing inside of her. *What if?* was all she could think.

Brad watched the emotions play across his wife's sweet, childlike face. She would never be able to hide anything from him. Her face told the whole story. He knew just what she was thinking. Leaning forward he pressed his lips softly onto the rounded bump of her belly. Then moving upwards he kissed her very thoroughly. When he was done, there was no question that she had been kissed.

"Good morning Mrs. Conroy."

"Good morning to you Mr. Conroy. How did you sleep?"

"Well to be honest with you, I'm not used to sleeping with anyone. I've always had the bed all to myself. I discovered last night I married a covers hog. I think you don't like to share. I may have to punish you immediately." He gave her a wicked grin.

"Punishment is in the eyes of the beholder." She giggled. Throwing the back of her hand up to her forehead she ordered, "So go ahead if you must."

Their morning was spent discovering who they were as a couple. The precious moments that would become the building blocks of their intimate relationship. The base that would define who they were together as man and wife.

As the clock rolled past noon, their bellies began to rumble. They had snacked sometime in the middle of the night from a basket of food Angelina had sent with them. Now they were looking for real food.

Noelle jumped out of bed and headed for the shower, "First one done chooses the restaurant."

Brad, quicker than she could draw breath, jumped out of bed and grabbing her tossed her gently back onto the bed. The battle was on. Each one fighting for the victory moment. In the end they decided to share the shower and lunch again was postponed.

Ravenous now, they found a quaint little family restaurant on the water front. Brad had booked a hotel for them on Lake Michigan. As they sat and watched the waves roll in, they ate burgers and fries. "What would you like to do first?" He asked her.

"I would love to walk the beach." She answered.

"Are you sure? It could be a little brisk."

"I'm not afraid. Are you chicken?"

"You are a little sassy this morning. Okay we'll walk. But there's a gift shop across the street. I say we go and buy sweatshirts first. The last thing I need is my wife getting sick on our honeymoon." Brad planted a kiss on her nose.

"Are you sure? A gift shop isn't the best price on sweatshirts." Noelle questioned.

"That's my girl. Frugal. I like that. But today we do what we want."

"Can we afford to do that? I mean...I don't really know anything about our finances. Not that I'm prying. I just don't know what we can afford and what we can't."

"No. You are absolutely right. We're in this together. We need to both be informed so we can make wise financial decisions about our future."

Noelle tried to become very serious, "Well then let me start. I own my car and I have $332.00 in my checking and some cents. I don't intend to spend it all in the same place." She stifled a laugh.

"Really? I would have thought your dowry would have been bigger than that. Not even a cow or a sheep for trade?" Brad shook his head as if it were shameful.

"Seriously, I don't have to have a lot of stuff. We can save our money. We don't even know what we're going to need for the baby. You know that isn't very far away." Noelle affectionately stroked her belly. She loved the feel of the rounded area that for now cuddled this child. Until recently, she hadn't allowed herself to enjoy the changes that were happening to her body. Until Brad's proposal, she wasn't sure she would be able to raise her child. In one short week everything in her life changed. She now had a husband and a future lay ahead for her baby; a future she would be a part of. Praise God for the way He had given her the desires of her heart.

"We aren't broke just yet." Brad said. "I haven't been a spender. Remember, I've been working the farm for a lot of years. I'm a saver. We're comfortable. I only have a few more payments to make on my truck. I have about $8000 in the bank and I have feeder calves that will be going to auction this month. We're very comfortable. We have a nice little nest egg to start our life."

He continued, "If we decide we want to buy a house, we can. If we want to stay at the farm for a while, we have that option. Mom's excited we agreed to the room change and that we're planning on staying at least for a little while. She's hoping we're going to stay past the coming of the baby. She can't wait to get her hands on Baby Girl." Brad gave her that *'know it all'* look of his.

She was enjoying their shared camaraderie. Learning the many facets of her new husband was proving to be very enjoyable.

"I'm comfortable at the farm. Plus, I'm sure it will make your life easier if you aren't having to come from somewhere else to do the chores that you need to do."

"That's my girl. Always so practical." Brad laughed. "Is that true of my beautiful wife? Are you always going to be the practical one of us?"

"I don't know if I'm practical. I didn't grow up having to worry about whether we could afford something that I wanted or needed. I asked and it just happened. However, Dad and Mom did make sure that we understood the value of a dollar and we were always quick to help someone who was struggling. They taught us lessons through conversation. We talked about everything. If someone we knew was in financial trouble, Dad would find a way to make it a teaching moment. We weren't frivolous, we just didn't have to be frugal. We had a comfortable life." Noelle paused in her stroll through memory lane.

"So, my new wife, where are you now in your financial thoughts?"

"Well...a few weeks ago I didn't know if I was facing taking care of myself or building a home for me and the baby. I was preparing to be completely independent. That's why I worked so hard at the Restaurant. I had to get ready for whatever the future held. It was a good time. It certainly taught me the importance of working hard and being prepared for life's changes."

"You worked too hard. You worked too many hours. Now you can just settle in and get things ready for the baby. Your life is about to change drastically. This can be your time for yourself. After all it will be years before you have time to yourself again. Especially if we are going to fill a house with rug rats." He smiled.

"Bradley Conroy, you just hold on a minute. I did not ask to be a kept woman; nor did I plan that I

23

would not work at the restaurant. I love what I do there and I like that I'm able to make your mom's life easier. Pregnancy is not a disease and I don't have to be babied just because I'm having a baby."

"Whoa there Nellie girl. Don't get your panties in a bunch. I was just trying to do something really sweet for someone that I love. If you want to work, then by all means work. The truth is, I didn't for one minute believe that I could talk you into relaxing anyway."

He smiled that irresistible dimpled smile and she melted.

They finished their meal laughing as they discussed less controversial topics.

Brad knew this for sure, there would never be a dull moment with his new little wife.

After lunch they did visit the gift shop and both purchased matching hoodies that showed the mitt of Michigan and outlined the Great Lakes.

The sandy beach was perfect. They rolled up their jean legs and chased each other up and down the lake shore. The water was freezing cold when the waves would catch them; but they didn't care. It was a beautiful day, full of sunshine and laughter. They both hated for it to come to an end. On the way back to their hotel, they stopped and ordered fish and chips to go. Deciding to have dessert first they stopped at the Dairy Queen and both ordered huge tin roof sundaes. How funny to find out they both liked the same kind of ice cream. They agreed it would make it easier when they were buying it by the container. Just another tidbit of information that Noelle was finding out about her husband. The idea of that still seemed so unreal to her. *Her Husband. Wow.*

After quick showers they sat on their deck with the fish and chips and watched the sun go down. It was beautiful across the lake. As the sun set, they were reflecting on the first forty eight hours as husband and wife. God was so good. They prayed and said, *"Thank you."*

✱✱✱✱✱✱✱✱✱✱✱✱✱✱✱✱

Back at the ranch, after the clean up of yesterday, Angelina, Genie, Aunt Debbie and the girls all sat curled up in front of a cozy fire. The girl talk had been wonderful and they were all dragging their feet; knowing that tomorrow they would be headed back to Atlanta. Without Noelle.

It was Debbie who voiced it first. "Why go back? What I mean is...If all of you love this area so much, why not move here? That way you would be close by when Noelle gives birth. You would be here to watch the baby grow. Your family is growing. Look what you have done with this marriage. Both of you have doubled your families. What do you really have going for you back there that couldn't happen here? A new change just might be the best thing for all of you."

The girls looked at each other and then at their mother.

Genie said, "The girls have their school. We have the house. What about my job?"

Instantly the girls chimed in together, "We would change schools."

Genie looked at them in disbelief, "You would want to leave everything you know and travel all the way across the country? It would mean starting all over with new friends."

"Yes!" They both instantly agreed. They couldn't believe their mom didn't think they would love to start

25

over somewhere new. A fresh start would be awesome.

"You're not serious...Are you?" She questioned both of the girls as they were noticeably getting excited.

"You bet we are." Anaya answered.

"We couldn't...I mean...The house. My job."

"Yeah...You're right. The house would never sell and you probably would never find a new job." Debbie mocked her sister.

"Oh my goodness." Angelina jumped in. "Noelle and Brad would love having you all here. Can you imagine what the holidays would look like? We would have huge family meals; great gatherings of fun. It would be wonderful. You could all stay here until you found a place of your own. We have plenty of room. I would love having you close. We could be grandma's together."

Genie smiled at Angelina. She knew just where to go for the direct hit.

"I don't know. That would be a huge decision; life changing. Not something we could decide without giving it some thought. This isn't the best market in which to sell a house.

Angelina just smiled, "God's market is always good."

"What about my job? Michael has been wonderful. He gave me the opportunity when, I'm sure, no one else would have taken a chance. What if I can't get another job?"

Always the voice of reason, Angelina said, "Well, I say let's pray about it. God always knows what's best and what we need. He would never lead us in the wrong direction."

Nissa said, "Agreed. And I'll pray...

Heavenly Father, we are coming to You tonight

26

for direction. You have joined our families together in a bond that cannot be broken. You know the distance that is between us now. We're asking for You to make a way for us to come together. We're asking that if it is Your will, You will set some things into place for that to happen. Lord, first we need our house to sell. Then we need You to supply a home here and lastly, Mom will need a new job. Father with You all things are possible. We trust You and we're waiting for You to direct our path. Thank You. In Your Son Jesus' name. AMEN Oh..Oh..PS: Could it happen quickly?"

"Amen." Everyone said.

Instantly the girls broke out in chatter. "Can you imagine? We could be here when the baby's born." Nissa said.

"Better yet. Let's not say anything to Brad and Noelle until we know for sure. Let's keep it a surprise. Won't that be fun. We could just show up one day on your door step and here we would be." Anaya said.

"Mom, let's look around at houses tomorrow. Just to see. Maybe we could find something right away." Anaya begged.

"Girls...Slow down. We haven't even sold our house yet. We couldn't buy until that happens.

"Our God isn't under any time restraints. I've been reading about the importance of speaking it forth. They say that the miracle is in your mouth. We release the angels to do their work when we tell them what we need. We need your house to sell and a new house to be found here." Angelina continued. "I have a friend who is a realtor. Why don't we give her a call and just see what she says."

"Yah. Let's do it. Come on Mom." The girls were instantly for making the call.

"Are you sure you want to leave the school you've always known? You would have to adjust. Do you really want to leave all of your friends behind? Nissa this is your senior year."

"Absolutely. Remember those were the same friends that spread all of the gossip when Dad left. We don't really trust any of them anymore." Anaya said.

"I'll finish. This is Spring Break. I only have a little over a month left of school. If God sells the house that fast we'll go to plan B." Nissa seemed more sure than Genie. But then she dropped the bomb. "Besides, I've decided I'm going to marry Eyan and go off to the mission field with him. It'll just make it easier if we're closer." Nissa announced very matter of fact.

The room went silent.

"Well 'Glory Be'! I'm going to get two daughters out of this deal." Everyone laughed at Angelina's statement. "When are we going to tell Eyan?" She asked.

"We aren't. He'll figure it out soon enough. We just have to get moved over here. You know...God will take care of the rest."

That being said, the discussion was over and Angelina was on the phone with her friend. The conversation went something like this. First she told a little about the needs and then she began to say: Really? No kidding. You can't be serious? How soon? When can we see it? Get out! Okay. We'll see you in thirty minutes."

Getting off the phone she said, "Well, you aren't going to believe what I'm about to say. Janet just got a listing for a house about five miles from here. Actually it's on the way to the restaurant. A professor from here is transferring to...You'll never guess where...Okay I'll just tell you...Your University. He wants to sell here as quickly as possible and buy there. Where? Where you live. If that isn't God affirming all of this I don't know what it is."

Everyone was speechless. They just sat looking at each other. No one moved. Could God have put all of this together that fast?

Nissa smirked, "Well I did ask in prayer if He could do this quickly. Just saying."

With everyone laughing Angelina started barking orders, "Well what are you waiting for girls? Let's get moving, we've got some house swapping business calling for our attention. We can't expect God to do it all by himself...Can we?"

Still in total disbelief, everyone jumped into motion at Angelina's orders.

When they got to the home, Angelina actually recognized the couple as patrons of the restaurant. She wouldn't call them regulars; but they had been in several times and as soon as she told them who she was they connected the memory also. "We really don't understand just how connected we all are." Angelina said as she warmly shook the owners hands.

The house was a lovely Victorian cottage style. It had high peaks and beautiful large windows. The doors were extra tall. The girls thought it was like walking into a giant doll house. There were four bedrooms with two and a half baths. Lots of storage space with a large living room and formal dining room. The kitchen was a good size with a cathedral ceiling. The basement was finished off and very comfortable. A huge surround sound entertainment system was built in and the girls were excited to learn this would stay with the house.

They talked about the move for this couple

to Atlanta. They thought it as unbelievable that both families were actually wanting to just change locations. The timing was perfect. Genie tried to describe their house to Professor Lee and his wife Patty. It helped that the girls could show them pictures on their phones that had been taken in the house over Christmas. It gave them a little bit of an idea what the house looked like. The professor's wife thought what she could see was lovely. She wanted to know when they could look at it?

"We're going home tomorrow. Any time after that would be fine." Genie still couldn't believe how all of this was playing out. But then, she was learning not to doubt God. He was a "Big God".

"We could make the trip down next weekend." Offered the man who said they could call him Professor, "If that would work for you?"

"Absolutely, and you are more than welcome to stay at the house if you would like. I work for the Dean of Students at the University. Perhaps I could show you around the campus and give you a head start.

"You work for Michael Dunn?" Professor Lee asked in disbelief.

"As a matter of fact, I do. How do you know him?" Genie continued to be amazed.

"We go back years. We went to school together all the way through our college years." He chuckled. "Quite the woman's man you know."

"I didn't know. Maybe you had better keep those secrets to yourself. I'm not sure Michael would want me to know all of his dark past." Genie laughed.

"A wise woman who doesn't need to be in the middle of everything." Professor Lee said.

Angelina jumped in, "So if you're leaving Indiana U, maybe you know of some open positions that are in need of an excellent woman who could fill the job. Genie is going to need a new job when she moves."

"I could certainly do some checking. I could let you know next weekend if I found out anything." He answered.

"I would really appreciate your efforts. However, please don't tell Michael before I get there on Monday and let him know myself. I would hate for him to find out that way. He's been wonderful to work with. I'll want to make sure all of his needs are met before I leave." Genie was going to miss working with her boss. He had really taken a chance on her during a broken time in her life. She would always be grateful.

"Absolutely. All though I do hope we can get together while we're out there this weekend. I do miss him. I'm excited to have this opportunity to be close to him again.

"Well, let me see what I can work out. I love to have guests over. Next weekend is going to be so much fun. I can already feel it." Genie surmised.

Genie and the girls left the house knowing this was what they wanted. They didn't even want to look at anything else. They were that sure. Next weekend would decide a lot about the direction of their future. If Professor Lee and Patty were interested in their house, then this little plan could come together nicely.

Everyone headed back to Angelina's talking all at the same time. It wasn't long after and Aunt Debbie headed to the airport to return home. There was a renewed enthusiasm about this though. With the move they would be about five hours north of her home. Only about an hour farther than currently. God is good!

****

The drive home had gone by quickly. The three girls had literally talked the whole way. The excitement was building about the possibility of a move to Indiana. Nissa was thinking she would start looking at getting a college visit to Indiana U as quickly as she could arrange it. Her plan was to get online and see what they had to offer her in foreign languages. She could get her Associates Degree in something that would lead into a teaching degree. That would always be something she could use on the mission field.

Genie laughed as her daughter continued to make plans for a future with Eyan. "Nissa, have you even had a serious conversation with Eyan? Where is all of this coming from?"

"Mom...I'm trying to follow God's lead. Isn't that what we're learning? I knew from the first moment I met him God was going to bring us together. You don't have to worry. We've learned to wait on God and see how He works. Isn't it going to be so much fun watching how He does it?" Nissa was adamant.

Really, Genie thought, *who am I to argue with her?* One of the things they should have learned by now is that God has a way of making everything work out. Look what they saw after the prayer on Saturday. Within minutes they were on their way to look at the house of a professor who was moving to their own area and needed a house. They couldn't have thought of it working out that way if they had tried. She thought to herself, *How could we have lived for so many years without God at the head of our family.* She couldn't help but wonder... *What if? If they had surrendered control and found that relationship with Him, would their family still be intact? Would Gale still be in their lives? Would they still be living as husband and wife? Would he still love them?"*

32

"Mom! Where did you go?" Anaya called her back.

"Just marveling at the wonderful God we serve." She smiled at her youngest as she thought, *How different will her life be from Noelle's with God's leading.* The guilt started to well up inside of her. Recognizing it for what it was, Genie rebuked the devil that wanted her to live in captivity. *Stop it! You can't make me go there. Life is too precious and God is too good. He has a great plan for my lives. His word tells me so.* Genie took a firm stand. She made a decision to hold fast and she wasn't turning back now.

It was almost 10:00 p.m. when the car load of tired women pulled into their garage.

"Grab your suitcases and I'll get the snacks. We'll clean the rest up tomorrow. You guys get ready for bed. Tomorrow morning will come early. You have school and I'll be off to work." Genie thought about the conversation she was hoping to have with Michael. It was beginning to feel like her life was going to take another turn. Only this time she wasn't scared or sad. This time God was leading the way and she felt safe and cared for by the Heavenly Father who loved her more than anyone else ever could.

Kissing the girls good night, Genie climbed into bed as quickly as she could. It had been a fast week. She thought about all of the changes that had occurred in such a short time. They went to surprise Noelle; but the real surprise came from Brad when he asked if he could marry her oldest daughter. She had to admit...That one she hadn't seen coming. But then neither had Noelle.

Still, one week later and she had not only given her daughter away in marriage; but she had gained the most wonderful son-in-law anyone could have found.

If there was one thing she was sure about, it was that Brad loved her daughter. Even though Noelle was as surprised as anyone about the proposal and the quick wedding, Genie watched as her daughter relaxed and allowed herself to fall in love with Brad. It was like watching a flower that had been closed up tight, slowly open and blossom into the beauty God created it to be.

The newlyweds had called last night while everyone was still at the farm. They were having a great time. The exhaustion of running through the waves on the beach had sent them back to their room to relax. Both of them wanted everyone to understand how much it had meant for them to all be together during this last week. They were already sad that when they came home, we wouldn't be there any more. "Brad and I will count the days until we are all together again." Noelle had ended their conversation with words of love to her family.

Genie laughed at the thought that maybe sooner than the newlyweds knew, they would all be together again. Permanently.

On that pleasant thought, she fell off to sleep and slept the whole night. So different from the sleep of the last year. This was the sleep of a woman at peace with her life. God was so good.

★★★★★★★★★★★★★★★★

The week flew by with the girls working to make sure the house was presented in its best form. The Professor and his wife Patty would be coming on Saturday. They had taken Genie up on her offer to spend the night at the house.

The girls were back in school and Nissa was preparing to finish her year strong. Neither of the girls

34

were playing softball this year. They had wanted to keep their time open so they could go see Noelle. Genie had felt bad at first about their decisions. Especially for Nissa because it was her last year to play. However, she was really beginning to understand that both of her girls had distanced themselves from the kids at school. There had definitely been a broken trust line. Not that they didn't have friends, they did. It just seemed like they weren't especially close to any of them any more. That in itself was a perfect reason to give them a fresh start somewhere new. Moving may be just what God saw they needed.

Saturday morning dawned with the excitement of their company coming. Everyone was awake early, breakfast was finished and the kitchen cleaned up. The weather outside was dreary; but the atmosphere inside was energized. Candles were glowing all around. There were fresh flowers on the tables. The smells began to blend together into a delightful aroma. The house was welcoming and putting forth it's best appearance. Nothing new here. Over the years many parties had been hosted for Gale's office in these very rooms. The house had known much laughter during those times. Genie had a knack for entertaining. Gale would proudly announce that Genie had done all of the preparations. She could still remember the feeling that would sweep through her when he would acknowledge her hard work. He would say, "She never uses a caterer; this girl of mine makes all of the food. The decorations are her own creation." The the best part would be when he would put his arm around her, give her a kiss in front of everyone and proclaim, "let's all say 'thank you' for everything Genie's done for us tonight." Everyone would applaud and Genie would bask in the pride of her husband. Who would have known he was living a double life? Surely not her.

But today, none of that mattered. She and the girls were ready and waiting. During the week their excitement had been building. They were already making plans to move. The thoughts of living by Noelle and Brad when the baby came and being an active part of all of their lives consumed their thoughts. It was becoming harder every day to keep the secret from Noelle. Several times in phone conversations she would ask one of them, Is everything all right? You seem funny."

"Fine...Everyone is fine. We just miss you guys." The answer would always stop her questioning. She understood because she missed them also.

This weekend would be the determining factor on how quickly this move was going to happen. Both homes were in selling order. Both were in good repair and ready to market. Gale had always insisted on taking care of what he owned. When something needed to be fixed, it was fixed. He always stressed it was important to take care of what he had worked hard for. It would have better marketable value. "You just never know when you need to make a change." He was always planning for the next big promotion. His promotions came quickly; yet had always kept them here in the main office.

Genie had checked with the attorney this week to make sure they could sell the house without any problems. He had reassured her the house was hers free and clear. She was able to make all decisions on her own. He even said if she needed any assistance with the house, he would be more than willing to help. Now here they were waiting eagerly for the couple whose decision could change their lives yet again.

The morning had dragged by and all of them watched the hands on the grandfather clock that chimed on the hour. Lunch had been a quick snack and the girls were upstairs doing something in their rooms. The quiet of the house was beginning to get on Genie's nerves. She went over to the stereo and began to pipe soft background music through the house. It only added to the relaxing atmosphere. She looked around her and felt a sharp pain. Was she really going to walk away from the home she and Gale had built for their family. Instantly fear shot through her. What was she thinking? She couldn't do this. How could she walk away and never look back. This was where she had raised her girls from babies, the best times of their lives had been lived between these walls. Gale had loved her here.

Then came that soft voice in her head and that feeling of warmth in her heart, *"My daughter hears my voice and feels my love for her"*.

Instantly Genie calmed, "Thank you Father for Your gentle reminders. I can and will do all things through Christ who strengthens me."

The doorbell, pulling her out of her mental wanderings, chimed softly, and Genie threw up a quick prayer as she walked to the door, "Here we go Father. This move is in Your hands. Do what You will with our lives.

Opening the door with her most welcoming voice she said, "Good Afternoon!" Genie motioned Professor Lee and Patty into the house as the girls came bounding down the stairs. "We're so glad you decided to spend the weekend with us." She smiled a heart warming smile.

Patty answered, "We're excited to be here also. I've had such an eagerness to see more of your home. The pictures the girls showed us certainly tickled my curiosity."

"Well let's get you settled in your room and we'll

take the grand tour. I hope you haven't eaten yet. I made plans for Michael and his wife, Chelsea, to join us for dinner tonight. I thought we could have some snacks to hold us over. They should be here around 6:00.

"Marvelous." Professor Lee was really pleased. "I had wanted to call him; but wasn't sure if you had spoken to him about leaving."

"Oh no. I spoke with Michael first thing Monday morning. I wanted to give him as much time as possible to find someone and make a smooth transition. He wasn't very happy with me until he heard the rest of the story. Then all he could do was laugh. His comment was, "Darn that Lee. He stole another one from me.""

Professor laughed.

Patty and Genie's looks told him that neither woman understood the joke.

"Apparently Michael didn't elaborate on the meaning of his statement?"

"Nope. When I asked he just said, 'Ask Casanova' and walked into his office chuckling."

With a smirk on his face he answered, "Let's just say that I stole something from him and we should both be happy she got away."

Grasping the reality of what he was saying, they all nodded in understanding.

"Well enough of that story. Perhaps we should let you and Michael journey through that memory together." Genie suggested, "Let's go upstairs and get you settled into your bedroom.

Genie and the girls had decided they would put the Professor and Patty in Noelle's room. Her old room had it's own bathroom. Nissa and Anaya's rooms shared a bathroom between them.

Nissa opened the door and stood back for the

couple to walk in. "Oh how pretty" Patty said. The girls hearts soared. During the week they had boxed up all of Noelle's stuff and stacked everything in the basement. A fresh coat of paint had been applied to the walls and with a new bed cover, some new curtains, and a few new pictures, the room looked very inviting. They had placed fresh flowers in a vase on the end of the dresser and beside it a small bowl of fruit with some chocolates and packets of mixed nuts. They had placed fresh bottles of water and cups. On the bed side stand was a new lamp with a shade that matched the curtains. The room was quaint and welcoming.

"Make yourselves at home. We want you to feel free to explore anything and everything about the house." Genie said as she helped them bring their bags into the room.

"This is more than gracious." Professor Lee said turning to Genie.

"Making a move like this is as important to you as it is to us. It needs to be right for everyone involved. Gale always insisted on keeping our house in order. I don't think you will find anything that isn't in top shape. If you do, it will be news to me and we'll get it fixed." Genie offered.

"Thank you Genie," Patty said taking her hand. "Shall we look at the rest of the house?"

"Of course. Follow me."

The two families spent the next hour or more looking through each area of the home. The Professor was very curious. The questions about the construction of the home were beyond her knowledge; however, she had remembered they had the original blueprints. Gale had asked for a copy of them when they purchased the house. Genie went into the closet in the basement where everything seasonal was stored. There in a hard cardboard tube were the prints. Rolling them out on the basement table, Professor Lee perused them thoroughly.

Leaving him to his studies, the girls all went back upstairs to re-look at the kitchen. Patty enjoyed entertaining also and she was very impressed with the kitchen. While she was browsing through the cupboard space, Genie was putting the snacks on the table. She had made little chicken salad dollops tightly wrapped in a fried pocket; vegetable sticks; fruit salad and homemade molasses cookies. There was hot coffee, tea and water with lemon slices to be added if anyone wanted. The table looked lovely.

Coming up from the basement, the Professor announced, "This smell is heavenly. If it smells this good I can't wait to sample your cooking Genie."

"Well thank you Professor. It really is very simple food. That's the dinner meal you're smelling. We're having beef roast smothered in onions and beef broth with red wine. I hope you'll like it. However, I'm afraid you're going to have to wait until Michael and Chelsea get here to find out if it's as good as you think it smells. I have a chicken salad snack prepared to hold us over until then."

"My dear, it all smells delectable and I can't wait to see Michael. However, maybe over the bite to eat you could answer a few more questions about the house?" Professor asked.

"Of course. Shall we go into the dining room." Genie led the way and everyone else followed her. Just make yourself at home. Professor could you offer thanks for the meal?"

"It would be my pleasure."

As each one found a place at the table, the
40

Professor began to pray.

"Father, we thank you for this day and the opportunity to spend it with such a lovely family. The beauty of Your kingdom is evident in the flowers on the table and the magnificence of Your bounty is made aware to us in the food that has been so lovingly prepared. Thank you for Your mercy that is new every day. Amen.

Nissa and Anaya sat quietly listening as Genie and the Professor talked back and forth about the house, the land and the possibility of what swapping houses would look like. They were becoming more and more excited about the direction the conversation was going. The Professor's wife, Patty, loved the house. The Professor was impressed with everything he had seen. They were laying out the comparisons on paper and considering what would be a fair value for both homes.

When the meal was done, Professor Lee had made an offer to swap homes plus he would give her $20,000 extra. The homes were very similar in size and age; but he felt like location made Genie's house worth more on the market.

Genie had a hard time not showing surprise. She never had expected to walk away with money in her pocket. The extra money would cover the expense of having their possessions moved to Indiana. This truly was God at work and it confirmed to her that He had put His endorsement on her and the girls making this change.

After a hand shake and an agreement that both parties were happy with the arrangement, the Professor said, "You know, I would have gone a little more if you had insisted."

"You know, I would have been content with an

41

equal swap." Genie grinned and everyone else laughed.

****

Michael and Chelsea arrived exactly as expected. It was clear to see the close bond between the two men. Apparently Chelsea and Patty had become quite familiar with each other over the past years.

The women sent the men to the den to catch up while they went into the kitchen to finish up the last minute preparations for the dinner meal. There was much chatter as both families shared with Chelsea the news of their move.

"You know Genie," Chelsea said, "Michael's going to be so sad to see you go. He isn't keen on having to look for someone to replace you. He tells me it'll be almost impossible."

"I'll miss him very much. Michael was so kind to take a chance on me. I've enjoyed every day of working with him and the students. I can only hope I can find something in Indiana I will enjoy as much." Genie shrugged.

"Oh we forgot," Patty said out loud as every one looked. "We were supposed to tell you Professor Lee talked with a colleague of his who runs the Office of Public Affairs at Indiana U. He's going to have to replace his office manager in June. Professor told him about you and your work with Michael. He wants to talk with you next week."

Again Genie's head was spinning at the way God was working all of this out. "June would be perfect. That way Michael would have time to post my job and I could help the new person get acclimated in the position. Professor is wanting to make the house swap the end of May during the Memorial Day weekend. It couldn't have worked out better. I'm so amazed at the hand of God in every step of this move."

The girls were laughing, "We aren't." Anaya said.

"Nope. Our God is a great God." Nissa chimed in.

"You're right." Genie nodded. "Now let's get the men to the table and see if the Professor will think that roast tastes as good as it smells."

Chapter Three

Psalm 32:3

When I kept silent,

my bones wasted away

through my groaning

all day long

THE PHONE RANG AND SHAUNA ANSWERED ON THE second ring. She had taken the phone with her everywhere she went today just in case. In case Del called.

"Hello." She answered hesitantly.

"Mom?"

"Yes Honey. Are you okay?"

"No Mom. It's terrible in here. When is Dad going to get me out? I can't stand it one more minute." She could hear her adult son was on the verge of tears.

"Listen to me Del. This is serious. Your Dad is working on some things trying to help you; but hear me, you have to calm down. You have to get a grip on yourself. What happened in the courtroom today can't happen again. Do you understand what I'm saying?"

"Yes...yes. I just lost my cool. I know it was a wrong way to handle the judge. I'll be better. But can't you get me out on bail?"

"Apparently not. Your Dad would have already done that if he could. What you did today didn't help at all. Tomorrow there is going to be another arraignment. We've brought the attorney different clothes so Judge Marshall will see a different young man. You're going to work on keeping your cool and being respectful to the people in authority. Do you hear me? I'm serious about this Del. This isn't a game that's going to go away. We're going to have to walk through this struggle. We'll be by your side. But you're still going to have to do this." Shauna hoped she was getting the point across. This was serious. She wanted him to understand. She also wanted him to know how much she loved him. She had probably loved him to a fault.

"Del, we're going to be okay. I love you and your dad loves you. We will be okay together. Right?"

"Right Mom. All right. I'll be better. I promise. Just do what you can to get me out of here. I can't stand it. I really can't." An officer tapped Del and motioned for him to wind up the call.

"I have to go Mom. I love you both. Tell Dad, well tell him I'm sorry."

"I know Del...We know."

Del could hear his mother crying.

The line went dead and Shauna sank into the wing backed chair beside the phone. She sobbed. Her heart was breaking. Her only son was in a situation that couldn't possibly be true. It just couldn't. She didn't know what she would do if it were.

****

The officer who had tapped Del on the shoulder pointed back in the direction of the cells. Walking inside, he heard the cell bars clang as they locked shut. Del was thankful for the reprieve of having no one in the cell with him. He wasn't sure he could have stood being locked down with a stranger.

How do you think those girls felt when you abused them? What do you think they live with everyday?

Del wasn't sure where that voice in his head was coming from. It wasn't helping though. He didn't want to think about those girls. Not any of them. They got him into this trouble. If it weren't for them, he would be...

Where? Where would you be? At another party? Drugs, alcohol, unsuspecting women? Is that

46

where you would be?

Stop it. I don't want to think about it. If it wasn't me, it would be someone else. I didn't mean any harm by it. They were at the parties too. It isn't like I pulled them off the street and raped them behind a tree. They came knowing what was going on at the parties. They liked it or they wouldn't have come.

What if you had a sister and someone treated her like that? Would that be okay with you? What if some man treated your mom the same way? Would it be okay?

My sister or mom wouldn't put themselves in a position to be treated like that. They would have more class than that.

So they would have class; but you would not?

Stop it. You're twisting my words. I don't know. I can't think. You're looking at this all wrong. I was just at a party. People have sex at parties. Girls know that when they come.

You drugged them! They didn't have a choice. You took that option away from them. Are you so insecure you have to force women? They didn't have control over anything that happened. They didn't choose you willingly.

Stop talking to me. You don't understand. It's what happens at college. This isn't anything new. Guys have been doing this to girls forever.

Well these girls are going to put a stop to it with you. You're in big trouble now. There's going to be proof you did what they say you did. You left your own evidence for the hospital to find.

Del started to sweat. He was going to be caught. His mom and dad were going to find out. His life would be ruined. He didn't know what to do. Sinking...I'm

47

sinking. If I were in water, I would drown. Del could almost feel the air being sucked out of him. He couldn't breathe.

Out loud he yelled, "There must be a way for Dad to fix this. He has to. What do I do? Who do I talk to?" He screamed, "Someone help me."

****

Pastor Preston Cronkhite was driving to the jail to make his rounds for the second time this week. The fatigue of the day was weighing in on him. It had been a long month. One of the families of his church had lost their father and loving on them was wearing on his spirit. If he hadn't felt like this was such an important ministry, tonight he would have just gone home and spent time with his girls. At twelve and ten he was feeling the pinch of time slipping away. They were growing up before his eyes and he had so much yet to teach them. Lessons like: The world is a hard and ugly place. Evil lurks around every corner. Satan doesn't show himself right up front, he's always disguised. The burden of protection was hanging heavy on Preston's shoulders. Most days he could ward it off. But, when he was tired; then he felt the pressure. Today was one of those days.

A quick stop at the jail just to make sure everyone was okay was still in order. He liked to talk with new inmates right away. It was important to get to them while they were broken and start planting God seeds. He never knew how long they would be there. Preston always felt the burden of time. He never wanted to miss an opportunity to reach a soul.

Entering and scanning his card, he was greeted by the officers and staff on duty tonight. Preston had worked hard to develop a relationship with the jail employees. Especially those who had been here for a long time. It's easy to become hardened when you deal with all they had to see everyday. He likened it to being on the battle field. You began to see them as the enemy. Fatigue can over take you. Attitudes can change. Preston watched for those signs. The court system had hired him to counsel with anyone that displayed a breaking down of their spirit. He was regularly brought in during exceptionally hard cases to talk with everyone involved. Preston liked to keep a close eye on those he saw on a regular basis.

The officers knew why he was there and they would try to keep him informed when someone new came in they thought he should talk to.

As he walked through the body scanner, Officer Kent met him on the other side. "Hey Pastor, thought you'd want to know we got a new guy in yesterday. Charges are going to be pretty bad. Accused of date rape. Fraternity parties, alcohol, drugs, multiple girls coming forward. Rich boy. Thinks daddy's gonna make it all go away. Cell block 'C'. #23."

"Thanks. I'll be sure and check in on him after I make a few of my regular rounds. How about you Kent? Are you hanging in there?"

"Oh...I'm doing okay. I have a happy, healthy family. My bills are paid and there's food on the table. Life could be worse...Right?"

"You finding time to read God's word? How about your church? Everything good?"

"It's all good Pastor. It's all good. But thanks for asking. And you? You doing okay? You hanging in there? Cause I know sometimes the days can be long for you."

49

"It's going to be the best year ever. The Christian's finest hour. Lives are going to be changed."

"Amen Pastor."

"Take care Kent."

"Thank you sir."

Cell block 'C'. #23. Preston's spirit sank a little. Time at home was looking further and further away. He was having thoughts of spending time with his girls and instead his time was going to be spent with some guy charged with doing unthinkable things to other fathers' little girls. Somehow today it just didn't seem fair.

Making rounds and touching base with some of the guys who had been around for awhile went pretty smooth. One of the young men had really grabbed hold of the gospel and was teaching a Bible Study class during the day. The jail was very good about letting the inmates get together for studies. It was to their own advantage to do so. History had shown the guys who participated in those studies came back to jail less than those who didn't. The truth is, God changes lives. It's just that so many of these guys come from such dysfunctional lives that the odds are against them. Preston's pet peeve is that the churches did not appear to be doing such a great job of reaching the homes. He felt like it was really going to take a whole community working together to change lives. Some days he felt like the Lone Ranger and he didn't even have a Tonto.

As he entered Cell Block "C", the noise was deafening. He often wondered what all of this must seem like to someone who is a first time offender. He was being led down the walkway. Stopping at #23, he heard Officer Jones say, "Got a visitor."

The bars slid open and he heard them close behind him as he stepped inside. Lying on the bed was the young man whose life was tipping upside down. Assessing the situation, he noticed on the right side of his face it looked like tear streaks. Yet, the look on his face was very confrontational. His hair cut said he was used to expensive things. Though his hair was messy, you could see the quality of the cut. It takes money to make that happen. He must really be feeling out of his comfort zone.

Stretching out his hand he said, "Hey, Pastor Preston Cronkhite here. I heard you came in yesterday. Thought I would stop and see if there's anything I can do for you. Do you have any needs I can help with?"

Del looked at the Pastor. Pastor Preston could see the emotion playing across Del's face. Then in an arrogant tone came the reply, "I don't know. What can you do for me?"

Pastor was amazed at the emphasis' he put on "can".

He replied, "Well, I can sit and talk for awhile. I can get you a Bible if you're interested. These days can be really long when you have nothing to do." Preston waited for Del to open up the door. He had learned a long time ago that barging right in didn't get him anywhere. There wasn't much trust in a setting like this.

Del said, "I don't know about all of that stuff. If it makes you happy I guess it would be okay."

"I have a Bible. It doesn't make me happy or sad if you choose not to get one," stated Pastor Preston.

The Pastor thought the statement took Del by surprise. Del must have thought Pastor would beg him to read the Bible. Not so. They have to want it.

"Okay. Fine. I'll take whatever you have," Del said as he positioned himself back on the bed.

Pastor leaned against the wall. Waiting.

Watching.

"You got something to say? Just say it." Del said.

"It doesn't sound to me like you're in much of a position to be a punk. I heard you got yourself in a lot of trouble. Heard those girls are yelling pretty loud." Preston taunted him...Just a little.

"Whatever. A man is innocent until proven guilty."

Preston whistled. "Pretty smart you are. You know all about the law. But do you know that there is a heaven and a hell and that we're all sinners saved by grace? Did you know there is a sovereign God who's watching all you do. He sees every move you make or have made? Did you know He loved you enough to send His son to the cross to die for your sins? Even though he was sinless. Now I don't know about you; but I don't want to suffer for any man I don't even know."

The Pastor waited for his response.

"So what do you want me to say? Hurray for Him. Thanks, for all of that," Del responded.

The look on his face made Preston want to slap him.

Instead he suggested, "That would be a great place to start. Start by figuring out it's not always about you. There are others involved in your life. What about parents? You got any?"

"Yeah, I have great parents."

"They must be really proud right now? This would be every parent's dream. You know...Get the call that says, 'Your son's been incarcerated in the County Jail.'"

"What do you want?" Del asked.

Preston looked straight at him and said, "I want

52

to help if I can. If I can't, I want to go home and spend time with my family." His answer even surprised him.

Del looked at him and said, "Then go. I don't care."

"Okay. I'm out of here. Good luck. I'm around a couple of times a week. If you change your mind, just ask for the Pastor. They know who I am. I'll be praying for you." And with that he called for the Guard and didn't look back.

Del felt totally alone again when he left. He wondered to himself, *Why didn't I talk with him. Anything would be better than talking with myself right now.*

✳✳✳✳✳✳✳✳✳✳✳✳✳✳✳✳✳

Following the guard back down the walkway, Preston wondered if he had been too abrupt with the young man. It was easy to see he was hurting. But it was just as apparent he wasn't ready to surrender and accept anything or anyone, not even God.

Preston wasn't even sure he understood how serious the charges were that had been brought against him. He couldn't help but wonder about where he had come from. One thing was sure, if he was found guilty, he knew where he was going and it wasn't going to be pretty. This young man's life had just taken a turn for the worst and it was going to get ugly.

Father, please be with this son of Yours. He needs You. Even if it hasn't become clear to him yet. Use me if You can. I'm willing. Give me strength to do what needs to be done. And Father, could you give a measure of strength to his parents? They must be sad. Help them to see Your hand in all of this. Amen.

Walking out of the jail and back to his car, Preston

wondered as he had so many times before, *What causes a young life to get so messed up? How does it happen? If they would just follow God's path, their lives would look so different. I sure don't want to get this wrong with my girls. The world is just waiting to snatch them up. You really need a lot of wisdom to lead a family in a better way. I want to raise them in such a way they know God and follow Him. That's what keeps the enemy away.*

Father help me please.

Those thoughts ran through his mind all of the way home and into his garage. He couldn't wait to get inside and grab those girls and let them know how much they were loved. It's so important for a dad to love his girls and for them to know. A wise man once told him girls need to feel the love from their daddy. If they don't they will find it from some other guy. He had made a decision right then and there no other man was ever going to take the place he was given in the lives of his daughters. They would know they were loved. He would tell them often. He would wrap his arms around them and make them feel safe. Then down the road, when the time came, they wouldn't settle for just any guy. They would find the men sent from God. They would be the special ones that had been created only for his girls. His girls wouldn't ever have to "settle" to feel love.

Preston made up stories about the girls finding their one and only man. He would tell them to his daughters before they went to sleep. Always they would have happy endings and God would bind his Princesses to their 'Knights in Shining Armor' with a cord of three. A cord of three was always stronger to withstand the attacks of the enemy. Preston would tell them the cord was a combination of them, their Knight and God.

54

The nights he didn't get to kiss them off to sleep never felt the same. This was his way of closing out his day and letting the ugliness he saw all too often fall away. God had called him to make a difference. This is the perfect place for him to start. Daughters needed their daddy's love and daddies needed to step up to the plate and be the men God called them to be. That was a life changing message and the best advice that Preston could give any new father.

What if the men in this world would all do the job they had been given from God? This society would look different if the next generation felt the love and support of the men who had given them life. The saying goes like this, "Any man can be a father; but only a special man can be a daddy." Preston couldn't help but wonder how lives would change if all children had a male figure in their lives, leading and directing. He was sure his job would look totally different.

God had seen the need for strong male figures. He created Adam and then gave him dominion over all of creation. God sits as the example of a loving Father. He loves us unconditionally. He knew we would need direction and He wasn't afraid to chastise us when we needed it. So He must have also known the guidance would have to be firm and corrective. Yet He wanted us to feel the love He has for us.

Preston wanted to get that message across to the inmates in the jails. He wanted them to know there's a better way. They were created for a life of abundance and that life can start right where they are at in this very moment. God will meet them right there. They don't have to do one more day on their own and it doesn't matter if they didn't come out of the best home. God just wants to make it better.

It was a message of hope Preston tried to deliver to each of the young men and women he saw. There was nothing more exciting than watching a life change right before his eyes. It was a good feeling to know another one was stolen away from the grip of satan.

Preston loved the opportunity to come face to face with those who were lost and offer them a new way. What bothered him was knowing when they left, they might not have anyone feeding into their lives to help keep them on the right path. The attacks of satan were relentless and it took a strong person to be prayed up and ready. They needed to be constantly in the Word of God so His Word could be building their faith.

Preston wanted them to understand a warrior isn't trained in the middle of the battle. He was to be built over time. In the war against satan, that preparation comes with building our spirit man to fight. One of his favorite scriptures that he loves to share with them is this, *Ephesians 6:10-18: Finally be strong in the Lord and in His mighty powers. Put on the full armor of God so that you can take your stand against the devil's schemes. For our struggle is not against flesh and blood, but against the rulers, against the authorities, against the powers of this dark world and against the spiritual forces of evil in the heavenly realms. Therefore put on the full armor of God, so that when the day of evil comes, you may be able to stand your ground, and after you have done everything, to stand. Stand firm then, with the belt of truth buckled around your waist, with the breastplate of righteousness in place, and with your feet fitted with the readiness that comes from the gospel of peace. In addition to all this, take up the shield of faith, with which you can extinguish all the flaming arrows of the evil one. Take the helmet of salvation*

and the sword of the Spirit, which is the word of God.
And pray in the Spirit on all occasions with all kinds of
prayers and requests.

He used this scripture often in his ministry in the
jails. It said it clearly. They have to be ready to battle.
The devil was going to attack. The problems of this
world would come from the powers of the dark world.
Satan was real. He really would come to kill, steal and
destroy. People would have to be prepared. There were
not enough people giving this message to these young
men and women whose lives were in chaos.

Occasionally Preston would get weary from the
battle and needed to be reminded of why he does what he
does. Someone saved his life one day many years ago.
He gave him the message of salvation and brought him
out of the pits of hell and into the light. If it hadn't been
for that friend during Preston's darkest days offering him
the light of truth, Preston could have taken his own life
and never had what he has today. God was a life changer
and he owed Him everything. So when he was tired,
he remembered that someone cared enough to reach him
when he looked unreachable.

Preston's mind traveled back to that time in his
history when the drugs of an unstable life threatened
to be the end of him. That final day would live in his
mind forever and even though God had forgotten his
sins, Preston purposely hung onto those memories. He
knew he was forgiven. He knew he could lay down
those memories; yet he remembered them so he could
understand the brokenness of the young men and women
he dealt with everyday.

Preston couldn't think about that day without
thinking about his friend, Matthew, who wouldn't take
no for an answer. Matthew was there when Preston

57

took the overdose of drugs. He was there when Preston grabbed the gun to put an end to the vicious cycle his life had become. Thank God Matthew had came with the vengeance of someone fighting to save a life. It was because Matthew wouldn't give up that Preston lived today. Even though Matthew was a new Christian, he had known enough to war in the spirit. He had known that was where the battle was raging. And fight he had. In the end, God won out in Preston's life and here he was today fighting for the souls of others who were walking where he had walked. Preston thanked God for Matthew everyday. Without someone who was willing to be obedient to God's call, another life would have gone to hell.

Sinner...You bet! Saved by grace...Amen! He would always be eternally grateful for the fight in Matthew. For that reason alone, he had to fight for the others. Tonight he would rest and tomorrow would be a new day, a new battle.

Cell Block 'C'. #23...Tomorrow is a new day. A day that the Lord has made. I will rejoice and be glad.

Chapter Four

Psalm 32:4

For day and night

your hand was heavy upon me;

my strength was sapped

as in the heat of summer.

Selah

WHAT A WEEKEND. GENIE THOUGHT TO HERSELF as she cuddled into her bed. The changes were happening so fast she was struggling to stay on top. Professor Lee and Patty were so excited about moving into her home and she and the girls were making plans to pack and move to Indiana. They were still keeping all of this a secret from Noelle. Nissa and Anaya wanted her to be surprised. Genie was sure she would be surprised... Shocked seemed more appropriate.

However, when the day quieted, Genie couldn't help but realize the home where Gale had brought their babies home to, where they had shared their love and been a family, was going to belong to someone else. And if she was honest with herself, maybe she wasn't as excited about leaving the house where she could hang onto her memories of Gale. But the girls...Well they were sure a fresh start was a good thing and God must be thinking the same way. After all, He was making everything happen so fast she was still having a hard time believing.

Tomorrow she would contact the number that Professor Lee had left for her. He had already made contact with Nolan Sheridan. His office on campus was looking for an office manager. It was the Office of Public Affairs. She would find out if it sounded like she would be a good fit. She wasn't going to start second guessing God. If this wasn't the job He had for her, He would send another one. Trust. That was what she was going to do. She thought about the memory verse she was memorizing. ***Proverbs 3:5 Trust in the LORD with all your heart and lean not on your own understanding; in all your ways acknowledge Him, and He will make your***

path straight.

Michael had given her a reference letter that was amazing. If she was in the position of hiring someone, she would hire just off his letter alone. It made her sound like "Super Woman". It almost made her sound too good. She could almost hear a future employer say, 'Surely no one is that amazing'. She had actually laughed when she read it in front of him.

"Who is this woman you're talking about?" She had asked him.

"You don't even know your own worth." Michael laughed as he shook his head. "This office has run like a fine tuned clock since you came. You even kept me on schedule. Ask Chelsea...That's an impossible feat. It isn't going to be the same without you; but the office that gets you will find out soon enough what a treasure they've received."

"Thank you Michael, for everything. I will say it again. You took a chance, you allowed me opportunity to spread my wings and use my gifts. Because of you, I began to find my way again. I'll always be grateful." With that said, she turned with teary eyes and walked out of his office, closing the door on yet another part of her life. All that was left for her to do was tidy up her unfinished projects and prepare the new person who would be her replacement.

Genie was about to drift off into sleep when her bedroom door burst open and the girls came in screaming.

"Mom!" They both yelled.

"My goodness. What is it?" Genie bolted up right.

"Look at this." They held the newspaper in front of her face.

Sitting up on the bed, she positioned herself.

Reaching over to the night stand, she turned on the light and reached for her reading glasses. Forcing her heart to slow, she took a deep breath and reached for the paper.

"I was scanning through the paper looking for clippings for a class assignment and I found it. Right here. Read this." Anaya said.

Genie, with the paper in her hands began to process what had upset the girls. "Local Boy Arrested For Multiple Date Rapes At University", the title said. Genie quickly read what was written. She couldn't believe what she was seeing. A sick feeling began to churn in her stomach. Finishing the article, she looked at the girls."

"What about Noelle?" Nissa asked.

"I don't know." Genie silently acknowledged the fear that was also raging through her girls. How was this going to affect Noelle and her new life? Do they have to share what they now know? Genie wasn't sure what she should be thinking at this point.

"Girls," she said, "Let's pray and ask God to give us some direction with this?"

Taking hands they began to pray, *"Father, help us. We need You to show us what to do with this information. If this young man is the father of Noelle's baby, should we tell her? Or should we just leave well enough alone? Noelle and Brad are so happy. Do they even need to know any of this? Wisdom Father. Please. That's what we need. Wisdom. We'll wait for Your lead. Amen."*

"Mom." Nissa started to cry. "What if we don't tell her and she finds out later? Maybe that isn't fair either."

Anaya agreed, "The Bible says, *'The truth will set you free'.* I don't think we can keep this a secret. I'm

63

afraid we would feel worse down the road. Plus, I don't think I want that burden tucked inside of me."

Genie thought for a minute then said, "Okay. Let's sleep on it and see where God leads us in the morning."

"Okay." The girls both gave her a hug and headed off to bed.

Nissa turning said, "Mom, it's going to be okay, right?"

"Yes Nissa. God is our Rock. He's who we will trust. Off you go girls. School tomorrow. It's in God's hands. He will lead us in His timing. Good night for now."

As the girls closed the door, Genie knew sleep was the last thing she was going to find. Praying was more important. She needed to seek God for direction as she thought about Noelle. Then the anger inside of her began to rage. She knew it was wrong. Yet, she was only human. She would have to ask God to forgive her; but for now she would mull over the name...Delmyn Whitehall. "Did you rape my daughter?"

Genie thought on this well into the night before finally finding sleep. Tomorrow, God forgive her, she would find out all that she could about this man, Delmyn Whitehall.

****

After seeing the girls off to school, Genie hurried to work. She was relieved to find Michael was already in his office and was alone. Knocking cautiously on his door she heard, "Come in."

"Good morning. Do you have a few minutes?" She asked hesitantly as she enter the room.

64

Michael noticed her agitation immediately saying, "Absolutely. What's up? You're early even for you."

Standing from behind his desk, he motioned her to join him in a sitting area where he had two upholstered chairs and a coffee table. Genie positioned herself in one of the chairs and faced him defiantly.

"What do you know about Delmyn Whitehall?" She asked without hesitancy.

Michael could see the intensity of the emotion rolling across her face.

"Why do you ask?" He answered with a question. Something told him he needed to proceed with caution... For Genie's own protection.

"My girls read in the paper last night about his charges and his connection with the school."

"So you're concerned about the ramifications this may cause the school and the students?" It was obvious what he was seeing in Genie had nothing to do with the school or her job.

"I'm sure this will have aftereffects that everyone in this office will have to deal with; however, that isn't why I'm asking. Michael, I've come to you as a friend. I hope I'm not presuming too much about our relationship?" Genie looked deep into his being.

Her answer stunned him, "Can I ask why this has you so noticeably upset? As a friend."

"Michael, what I'm going to share with you no one else in this town knows except my girls." She paused.

"I understand. I assure you anything you tell me will stay between you and I in this room." He answered.

"You know Noelle was just married. She met a wonderful family, a family that we all believe she

65

was led to by God. We believe the marriage was God arranged. We also believe God took what satan intended for destruction and created new life. Noelle's new in-laws took her in when she had car trouble just down the road from their home. They nurtured her and loved her and helped her through a hard time in her life. It was during that time she made a decision to have the baby she was carrying instead of having an abortion. The baby she was carrying because of a drugged rape here at a fraternity house connected to this campus. When Noelle ran away from here, she was headed somewhere to abort the baby that was growing inside of her because of that rape. The girls and I didn't know. She was leaving to protect us.

It was beginning to make sense to Michael now. Genie was thinking the young man that had been arrested for the rapes that allegedly occurred on this campus was also the man who had raped Noelle. No wonder she was so upset.

"Genie, I am so sorry for what Noelle has had to endure. Also for what you and the girls have been put through. It isn't fair." He took her hand into his and patted it gently.

"Does Noelle know about any of this?" Michael asked.

"No. We aren't sure we should even tell her. She's just married to a wonderful young man who loves her and is excited about the baby. He isn't revengeful about the rape or the man who violated Noelle. He loves my daughter and the baby they are about to share. He cares about the life they are going to build together. Brad is a remarkable person; a strong man of God. He knew from the first time he met Noelle that God had brought her into his life. He feels like God created Noelle to be

66

his companion. He believes Noelle was the one woman made especially for him by God. Do we really want to complicate their lives with this?" Genie shrugged. "We don't know what to do?"

Michael pondered for just a moment and said, "If this young man really believes God sent Noelle to him, would knowing this situation change his beliefs?"

Michael paused allowing Genie time to consider what he had just said.

"I don't mean to lessen any of your concern for the problem. I understand your dilemma." He said as he continued to hold her hand. "I don't know the right answer. I can tell you what I do know. I know the young man who has been accused was charged with multiple rapes by multiple girls. They appear to have occurred at the fraternity house where he lived. He is an only child from a very wealthy family. What I have gathered from the professors who have had him in class, is that he is an arrogant, rich boy. Daddy's money bought him out of problems in the past; but I don't think money is going to fix his mess this time. I doubt it can be bought away. Of course I don't know anything about the case. However, the police have been in here and talked with me several times. I've given them assurance the University will cooperate with them in any way necessary. We want to get to the bottom of this as much as they do. It isn't going to be good publicity for us; even though we all know this happens on every large campus across the United States."

"What I know is this...It shouldn't have happened to my daughter. It shouldn't have happened to anyone's daughter...Ever. But it did. It was very real to Noelle. Now I have to decide how to proceed with what I know."

"Genie, this is just a thought. Considering the

fact you are a Christian family and you have all found the way of healing, I wonder if God isn't planning on using Noelle and your family in a positive way to help someone else who is walking through this same trial? If that's the case, is God using this to continue Noelle's healing? How would that be possible if she doesn't know? Just food for thought." Michael again patted her hand. "I really am sorry you're all having to deal with another challenge. God must see the strength in all of you that is growing daily."

"Michael, I'm thankful for what we have come through. Without the trial of Gale's leaving and Noelle's tribulation, we wouldn't have looked up to see who God was. But, how much more?"

"Genie, trouble that drives you to Jesus is a priceless treasure. It strengthens you. It transforms you. You have all experienced that."

"This is just my thought. God has brought you all this far. Don't stand in the way of His completing the path He has Noelle on. He'll continue to protect all of you, including Noelle. He's a 'Big God" who loves you all."

Standing, Genie headed for the door. Turning and facing Michael, she said, "Thank you for talking with me. Rest assured, I'll be very professional if I have to deal with any of this at work. I'll let you know what we decide to do about telling Noelle." Having said that, she closed the door and slipped into her work mode.

****

Noelle was humming to herself as she was preparing the salad bar at the restaurant. Everyday she was in awe of her wonderful life. She was married to a man who loved her and was caring and compassionate. His character was a lifestyle he lived, always. *Thank you God for directing my life and saving me from my running.* Noelle still shuddered as she thought about the choices she had been going to make. Putting her hand lovingly across her belly she soothed the little one that was apparently practicing the floor exercises yet to be performed. "Do you know how much I already love you?" She spoke out loud.

"You must be talking to me." Michelle said as she came up behind Noelle and tapped her on the shoulder.

"Oh goodness. You caught me." Starting to blush and then realizing that it was okay for her to enjoy the life that was becoming so present in her. Turning around Noelle grabbed her new friend. Laughingly hugging her she said, "My life is so wonderful, I can hardly believe it. Pinch me and see if I'm dreaming."

"Okay." Michelle said as she reached up and playfully pinched Noelle on the back of her arm.

"Ouch!"

"Nope you're awake." Michelle said.

"Meany. That hurt." Noelle pretended to pout.

"You're going to have to get tougher than that if you are going to bring that little girl out of there and into our world."

Noelle cringed at the thought of giving birth. She wasn't sure she was ready. "I've decided to just leave things as they are. This baby, boy...Or girl..Can just stay tucked inside. I think Baby will be easier to take care of that way." She laughed. "Plus, you'll all be heart broken if the baby comes out and isn't a girl. Shame on all of you. You guys are going to give him a complex before he's even born." Noelle scolded Michelle.

"I'm just going along with Brad. He's positive

we're all going to dance recitals and we'll be buying pretty little dresses. In fact, yesterday I bought the cutest pair of red patent leather shoes. They'll be too big for a while; but she'll grow into them." Michelle shrugged her shoulders. "I couldn't help myself."

Laughing, both girls went back to work so they could get ready for the rush hour which would start in just a few minutes. Noelle savored the moments she could laugh and enjoy her pregnancy. Never would she take for granted the precious gift Brad and his family had given her. Noelle's life was so different and because of their love and God's love for her, she would enjoy the wonderful months of her pregnancy and this gift of new life she had been given.

✶✶✶✶✶✶✶✶✶✶✶✶✶✶✶✶

The girls and Genie sat at the table eating the food that was left over from the weekend with their company. Genie could sense from their moods this problem had weighed on them all day.

Nissa was the first to break the silence, "Mom, what are we going to do about Noelle and this information?"

Before she could answer, Anaya said, "What if we call Brad and talk to him about it?"

The other two stared at Anaya. Silence surrounded them for moments as they all mulled over the new thought.

Nissa looked at her mom, shrugged her shoulders, and said, "Maybe? What do you think? We have to do something."

Genie rolled the idea over in her head for a few more minutes and then said, "Maybe we should do

70

exactly that...Call Brad. He has such a level head on his shoulders. This is a problem that could certainly affect his life. As the head of their family, it would make sense he should make this decision." Thinking for a little longer Genie said, "I think that's a great idea. Let's call Brad and let him know what we know. Then he can decide how to proceed and we'll support his decision one hundred percent."

Genie filled the girls in on the conversation she had with Michael that morning and they were even more sure Brad had to be told. Nothing good could come out of trying to hide the truth. They all thought it best Genie call Brad right after they finished eating. They were hoping she could talk with him without Noelle being there. It would be better for Brad to have sometime to process through all she was about to tell him. She wanted him to have time to pray and hear from God on how to proceed.

****

Brad had been working in the barn for a couple of hours when his phone rang. He wanted to ignore the ring. He was so close to finishing up and getting inside the house. Noelle was home and waiting for him. They had shared supper together alone. Eyan was gone off somewhere and his mom was sharing a meal with a friend who had recently had surgery and was living by herself. Brad loved those times when the two of them were alone together. But farm chores had called.

He had promised Noelle he would finish as quickly as he could; she had reassured him she was fine and was going up to the tub and take a nice, long bubble bath. She had worked a long day at the restaurant and was feeling it in her back. A soak sounded wonderful.

Having promised her a back rub when he was done, he was eager to fulfil his promise.

However, the phone was persistent and he put down the pitch fork and went over to answer it. Looking at the caller ID, he was a little surprised to see it was Noelle's mom. She rarely called his phone. They usually talked to her on Noelle's phone. He answered quickly before it went to voice mail.

"Hello."

"Hi Brad. How are things going today?" Genie was unsure how to even start the conversation she was going to have.

"Great. I'm in the barn finishing up a few things. Noelle worked a long day today and she's running up our electric bill, soaking in bubbles as we speak."

"Oh good. I was hoping to catch you by yourself."

"What? Is everything okay?"

"Yes. I just wanted to share something with you and let you decide if you want Noelle to know. We were hoping you would have sometime to pray about it alone before deciding what you wanted to do."

Brad puzzled at the strange conversation they were having. "Well you certainly have piqued my curiosity. What's up?"

Genie continued hesitantly, "The girls and I have seen an article in the local paper about a young college man who was arrested on rape charges."

"Yes...Go on." Brad knew already where this was going. He didn't know how he knew. He just knew.

"Brad, the man has been arrested for raping multiple girls at his fraternity house. They've all been drugged. Apparently there are several of them. Two of them went to the hospital. They pressed charges. After

they did that, the investigation has turned up many more."
Genie gave him time to process all she was saying.

"I see." Pausing. "You think this is the man that...Hurt Noelle?"

"The story, which is limited to say the least, does seem to be the same. The time line fits. The case is relatively new. It hasn't gone to trial yet. He was arraigned and is waiting trial in the county jail. The news is following the story closely. It's going to be in all of the papers. Working at the University, I have a little more information than most have. I don't think it's going to be very pretty. There seems to be more girls coming forward every day. Our office is in close contact with the police and helping with their investigation. We, of course, aren't told anything about the case. However, we are aware of the number of girls. Before it's done, I'm expecting there will be more young men arrested."

Brad was quiet as he was mulling over all he had been told. "I'm not sure what to do with this information. I agree with you. I think I should take sometime and pray. Were you planning on tell Noelle tonight?"

"No! To be honest with you, the girls and I haven't been able to come to grips with whether we want to tell Noelle. She's so happy. We didn't want to bring all of this up again. But...If it's spread all over the news; well, we were afraid she would see it. Is it better if you tell her or for one of us to let her know? Should she even be told? We've been struggling with so many of these questions. What we did agree on was that you're the spiritual leader of your family and if God is at work here, which He certainly could be, then it's only appropriate for you to have the information so you can pray." Genie paused as she wondered what Brad was thinking.

"Right, and thank you for that consideration.

Genie I think one of the questions is this, if she knows, will she have to make a decision to participate in the investigation?"

Genie knew that would come out sooner or later. It was one of the reasons she didn't want Noelle to find out what was going on.

Brad continued, "Does she have a duty here to step forward and either help the girls or help the accused man? I'm assuming that being pregnant would do one or the other."

The phone line was silent while both parties began to accept what direction this conversation was taking. Neither of them wanted to consider what it would cost the person they loved.

"Brad, did I do the right thing by calling?" Genie asked.

"Absolutely. We have to just figure out what God wants us to do now. I will pray about this and then I'll let you know what I think God is directing us to do. Will you do the same on your end?"

"You know we will. It was the first thing we did when the girls brought it to my attention. I'm sorry Brad."

"Listen. God always has a plan. Remember this, God loves the man who did this as much as He loves us. We'll work it all out. We'll all be okay because of Him. Hear me?" Brad waited for her to answer.

"Yes. Thank you for letting us lean on you. We need a man's strength to get us through all of this mess."

"We are family. I'm here for all of you. We'll see where God is going to take us. Are you guys okay?" Brad's loving nature came forward.

"We will be. As long as we know Noelle is okay." Genie said with tears running down her checks.

"Noelle is strong and courageous. She gets that from her mother. You've done an amazing job with your girls. Noelle is going to be just fine and so will all of you. God and I will see to it. Okay?"

"Okay." Genie took a deep breath.

"Would you like to pray together? Are the girls right there?"

"They are and we would love to pray with you."

"Why don't you put us on speaker phone and we'll do this all together." Brad suggested.

Genie did as she was told, "Okay. We're ready."

"Father God, we come seeking wisdom. You know what needs to be done. We ask that You make the way clear to all of us. We want to do the right things and we just need You to confirm what those are. We are willing to be obedient. Protect Noelle through all of this and keep her and the baby safe. Father, we come against any interference the enemy may have planned. Our family is protected by You. Your word says, "No enemy formed against us shall prosper. You are our Rock and our Refuge. In You we will trust." Thank you Father. Amen"

"You all okay?" Brad asked again knowing the girls were listening.

"Yes." Nissa said.

"We will be. Thank you." Anaya answered.

Genie asked, "Brad...Are you okay?

"I'm fine and don't worry...Noelle will be also. God and I will see that she is."

Genie asked one last question, "Brad, you will let us know what you're going to do before you do it? Right?"

"Sure will. Keep praying. As soon as God confirms it between us, we'll move. Love you guys.

Now...Don't worry. God is in control." With that, they all said their good-byes and hung up.

Brad went to the open door of the barn and looked out at the stars. The glistening of the night sky reminded him again that God was bigger than all of their problems.

Falling to his knees and looking to the heavens Brad said, *"Even so...I will trust you."*

Spending a few more minutes in prayer, Brad finished cleaning the stall, closed up the barn for the night and went to his waiting bride full of love and hope for the future. Resting in the assurance that God was in control, Brad knew all he had to do was wait for God's timing and direction. Life was so much easier when you didn't have to figure it all out by yourself.

Chapter Five

Psalm 32:5

Then I acknowledged my sin to

you and did not cover up

my iniquity.

I said, "I will confess my

transgressions to the LORD--and

You forgave the guilt of my sin.
                                    Selah

"ALL RISE." THE COURTROOM CLERK ANNOUNCED with a booming voice. "The Honorable Judge Owen Marshall presiding over the case of State of Georgia vs. Delmyn Whitehall. All present and accounted for." The Judge entered the courtroom from his chambers through a door behind the large wooden desk.

Delmyn wasn't impressed. He didn't think the Judge and him were ever going to hit it off. Maybe someday down the road when this was behind both of them, the Honorable Judge Marshall, would come crawling to Delmyn begging for money. Huh! He'll see who is in control then.

"Be seated." Judge Marshall banged the gavel down. Looking directly at Delmyn the Judge addressed Tempo Mohan. "Mr. Mohan, I am assuming you have instructed your client as to the proper etiquette for my courtroom."

"Your Honor, Mr. Whitehall has been informed of the rules of acceptable behavior. He has asked the Court to please forgive his irresponsible outbursts yesterday. He can only plead ignorance and duress under these circumstances. Never has he been in trouble before and the emotional trauma of his situation caused him to say and do things which were not in his best interest. He is asking the Court to accept his apology and not hold it against his character. He is truly sorry." Teo made a diligent effort to convince the Judge that the disrespect Delmyn exhibited yesterday was not a picture of his real person. "Your Honor standing before you is a humbled man."

Judge Marshall's eyes pierced deep into Delmyn and said, "I will not tolerate any disruptive behavior now or ever. It is my belief this generation of young people have too many who have lost the ability to give honor where honor is due. Mark my words. It will be to your clients detriment if I see any behavior that even leads me to question whether his apology is sincere."

"We understand and thank you Your Honor." Teo ended.

Delmyn was biting the inside of his lip the whole time that ornery old Judge was talking. He couldn't wait to get out of here and talk to his Dad. Surely they could stir up enough garbage on him to make a reelection run look impossible. In the end, Delmyn would make sure Judge Marshall knew where his problems came from. When he got out of here, no one was going to talk to him like that again. He would personally see to it.

Even with all of those thoughts running through his head, on the outside he looked very reverential and contrite. He played very well the part of being deeply sorry for having behaved badly. Truth be known, he had played that part many times over the years in front of his dad. Now as he looked back, it did seem he had gotten himself into a few uncomfortable situations. Although this is really the first time the problem wouldn't just go away. Delmyn was thinking, *Really Dad. You need to work a little harder.*

He felt the nudging of Teo Mohan dragging him back from his wanderings. *Focus Delmyn. Focus.* He thought to himself.

"I asked," Judge Marshall said, apparently for the second time, "How do you plead?"

"Your Honor, I plead not guilty." Delmyn answered.

Pulling his mind back into the here and now, his ears perked up as he heard the Prosecuting Attorney, Laura Lynn Lyndstrum, say, "I believe because of the financial potential in the family, Mr. Whitehall is a flight risk. I feel, under the circumstances, he should continue his incarceration in the county jail."

"Your Honor!" Teo sounded shocked. "Mr. Whitehall's record stands for itself. It is without blemish. This is his first offense. Never has he been in trouble before. For Prosecutor Lyndstrum to request him to continue his incarceration is without precedence. It is unreasonable and uncustomary. And may I remind you this family is an established pillar in the community." Teo professed adamantly.

"Yes, Your Honor, an established family who has enough money to make their only son's problems go away."

Delmyn was beginning to realize they were talking about sending him back to jail. Panic seized him. He couldn't go back. Not now. Not ever.

Teo countered with, "Still you have to look at the criteria of past practice. Regardless of the charge, this is still a man with a spotless record. I need not remind you this man is innocent until proven otherwise."

"Your Honor, when we present our case the State is going to paint a picture of a man who does not have a spotless record. His life will look very different. We will show you this is a troubled young man who has been in difficulty too many times; but because of family money has an expunged record. We believe, we are looking at a man who has been a perpetual problem to society; yet has been taken care of by parental intervention."

Keefe Whitehall sat with his head bowed. The grief that was flowing through every part of his body was almost overwhelming. He could feel, Delmyn's mother's body quiver beside of him as she gently cried. *How did we do this? We just loved him so much.* He thought to himself as he gently stroked the woman with great sorrow sitting beside him. The world around them seemed to stand still yet spin out of control all at the same time. *I can't stop this Delmyn...This time I can't stop this from happening.*

Delmyn thought to himself, *This prosecuting attorney is going to have to go down along with the Judge. Dad is going to have to get rid of both of them.*

"Your Honor..."

"Enough Mr. Mohan. I have made my decision. After your client's display in my courtroom yesterday, I will be forced to take into consideration the possibility that Mr. Whitehall may have a covered up past. His display here did not speak well of his character. Though he had you speak words of apology, he leaves me to wonder at his sincerity. So that being said, it is my decision Mr. Whitehall will remain under lock and key at the Atlanta County Jail until this case comes to trial. Trial date to be set according to Court availability. Officer remove Mr. Whitehall. Bailiff...Next case."

And the gavel was struck and Delmyn's life turned upside down. He was speechless. Staring at his attorney he threw his hands into the air and said, "What happened?" Immediately an officer of the court was beside him.

"You've angered the Judge after yesterday's performance. We're going to have that hanging over our heads from this point on. I'll be over to see you in a few days. Until then make good use of your time; show yourself to be an impeccable inmate. No screw ups. Exemplary." Teo turned as if to dismiss him.

The officer, taking his arm, began to guide him forward as he steered him towards the door he had entered earlier. Delmyn stopped and started yelling... "NO! NO! I WON'T GO! NO! I CAN'T DO THIS!"

The officer began to forcibly push him towards the door. He resisted.

"NO! NO!"

"Son, don't do this to your mother. You are breaking her heart." The officer whispered into his ear.

Stopping...Delmyn looked up and for the first time saw his mother and father sitting in the back of the room. His mother was draped across his Father's lap and her shoulders were shaking as she silently sobbed.

Stunned, he yelled, "I'm sorry Mom. I'm so sorry."

She looked up, distraught, as the court room officer continued to push her son through the door and it swung shut.

That was the picture Delmyn took with him to the cell. The look on his mother's face was total devastation. Old. He had never seen his mother look so old. Laying his head down into his hands, he cried, *What have I done. Forgive me Mom. Forgive me."* For hours he cried until there were no more tears.

****

A few days had gone by since the call Brad had received from his mother-in-law. Though she had talked everyday to Noelle, no mention had been made of the reason for the call that night. He had been in no rush. He knew God would have an answer in His time. He had been weighing all of the consequences and always the same answer surfaced. The wise man built his house upon the firm foundation. Foundations of sand will eventually tumble and wash away. Build on rock. Build on righteousness. Build on truth. Brad was listening to God's direction. Brad knew what he had to do. He was also smart enough to know this was going to be the hardest thing Noelle had ever done. But as her husband, he was going to help her face her demons. Together they would cast them away.

He also knew they could be opening up doors that could cause them heartache down the road. He knew by coming forward and reporting the pregnancy, they could be opening doors about a father's rights.

God always called out unrighteous behavior. He was certainly big enough to protect the righteous. Brad also knew that life wasn't just about Noelle and himself. He understood God was working out a plan in their life as well as in the lives of others that they didn't even know. Their job was just to trust and be obedient. They simply had to let God be God.

Brad intended to call Genie and the girls tonight before he came in from the barn. He was going to tell Noelle before they went to bed, during the time that was always theirs alone. Those moments before going to sleep when they cuddled into each others arms and the world only existed in their little room. He wasn't going to make a big deal of it. He would reassure her they were going to be all right. Yet he would impress on her the importance of helping the other girls who had been through what she had gone through. Maybe, if they would stand strong together, it would not happen to any more girls.

Noelle was sitting in the glider rocker Brad had given her as a wedding gift. She was looking out the window when he came into the room. Turning towards him she said, "Don't you just love seeing all the stars? They're so beautiful. I didn't see them growing up in a big city. The night sky was always illuminated. Isn't it amazing to think that a God who could create something so vast cares about our every desire? It just boggles my mind to think about Him loving me that much."

Kneeling down he kissed her tenderly. "The same stars that were shining down on me were shining down on you. And what boggles my mind is how He very deliberately allowed us to find our way to each other. Have I told you, Mrs. Conroy, how much I love you today? Because if I haven't, I have certainly been remiss."

"I would have to say you have; but maybe you need to say it more; just because I love to hear it."

Kissing her again he said, "I'm going to take a quick shower." Thoroughly kissing her again he said, "I will be right back. Don't go anywhere."

Noelle listened to the sounds he made in the shower. She could tell when he was shampooing his hair and she could tell he was shaving. She thought that was so funny. He shaved in the shower. There were so many little things she was learning every day about this husband of hers.

Brad was true to his word and with water beaded up on his back he knelt in front of Noelle as he kissed her once more.

"Ooooh!" She yelled. "You're still wet."

"Sorry. I promised you I'd hurry. It was faster if I didn't take a lot of time drying off." Pulling her to his damp body she giggled.

Pulling back he said, "Can we have a serious conversation for just a few minutes and then I want to get in bed and cuddle some? Okay?"

"Okay to the cuddling. It's kind of late for a serious conversation." She wrinkled her nose up at him.

Laughingly he tweaked her nose. "Late or not... We need to talk."

"Okay." She answered hesitantly.

Pulling up a chair so he was facing her he said, "Your mom called me the other night and asked me to pray about something. I have been and now I'm ready to share it with you so we can begin to pray about it together." He paused giving her time to prepare for what was about to come. "You know as long as we're together and in agreement, we'll be fine no matter what comes our way. Right?"

"Brad you're scaring me. What's this about?"

I don't want you to be scared. There's nothing to worry about. I will always be here to protect you, physically, emotionally and spiritually. That's a promise. You're stuck with me for better or worse, till death do us part." He smiled as he leaned in and kissed her one more time. The warmth of their intimacy was beginning to cloud his thought. Kissing her again he said, "Maybe we should just get to the cuddling and have this talk tomorrow."

"Oh no you don't Buster. You started this and now you have to finish."

"That's what I'm thinking about...The finish." He kissed her once more.

"Give. Come on." She tried to be stern as he continued kissing her and failed miserably.

Pulling himself back from his emotions, which were attempting to take over, he said, "Okay. So here is the deal. Your mom and the girls read in the paper, they've arrested a student at the University. He's been charged by multiple girls with rape. He is in the county jail awaiting trial. Apparently the girls' stories are the same as yours. Not all of them went to the hospital. However, some of them have and others have just come forward and told their same stories. It is fraternity parties where they have been drugged. It's going to be a big deal. The news is going to cover it nationally and they didn't want you to be surprised." With that he stopped and gave her time to process all he had said.

He could see her instantly tighten up. He didn't give her time to react. Picking her up out of the chair he carried her to the bed, laid her gently down and cuddled up holding her tight.

Whispering into her hair, he spoke soothing words of comfort, "It's going to be all right. We're in this together. You're the bravest woman I know, courageous and strong. I've married into a family of strong women. It's in your genes. I'm so proud of all of you. You amaze me daily."

"I'm not." Crying, she could barely get the words out.

Turning her to face him, Brad gently took her face into his hands and looking straight into her eyes he said, "Yes. Yes you are. Together, with God's help, we can conquer the world, at least the part He has given us." He was nodding his head to emphasize his point.

"What do you want from me?" The tears had slowed and were trickling down her face.

He kissed each tear drop that fell. "First, just listen to me. I want you whole and complete. I don't want anything standing between you and God. Forgiveness is a huge issue with Him. I know what I'm asking of you. I can see the fear that is trying to swallow you up and don't think I haven't considered the consequences of becoming involved in this investigation. I know we are opening our lives up for some family to think they may have some claim to our baby."

She gasped. She hadn't even thought about that aspect of all of this.

Before she could speak, he put his finger to her lips.

"I also know God has directed our every move. I'm equally sure He is leading this one. He wants you to face your demons. In helping these other women, you will be dealing with the ugliness you have tucked away inside. That isn't healthy. At some point, all of that will come bubbling up when you least expect it to rise. Taking you by surprise isn't the best way, it is satan's way. This way we deal with it right up front and nothing will come back to disturb us in later years. We'll let God be in control. We'll just go where He leads. He will take care of us and our baby. He has done a great job so far."

He watched the emotions roll across her face. He had been weighing all of this out for a few days. He wanted her to have as much time as she needed. He knew the pain he was asking her to face. But...He wasn't asking her to do it alone. He would be right there with her...And so would God.

"Brad, I'm scared. I don't know if I ever want to see that man."

"I know. Sometimes we have to do what we don't want to so we can become stronger. Our baby deserves the best we have to give. I don't want to live with the demons from that time. I say let's face them down and put them where they belong."

"What does that mean? Are you saying we have to get involved with the police? My name will be plastered across the papers. That's why I ran in the first place. I didn't want people to know." She was shivering.

Brad repositioned himself so he could cover her up.

"Don't leave me." She cried.

"I'm not going anywhere." Kissing her he said, "I promise. I'm not going anywhere."

As they lay together in the quiet of their sanctuary, Noelle though about how much Brad had to learn about her. One of those things was that she wasn't as strong as he thought. She didn't think she could survive facing her rapist. She didn't want him, or his family, to know about her baby. It was the end of April and the baby was due at the end of July. She didn't need this kind of stress now. Her life with Brad was good. Why couldn't they just be happy and learn how to blend their lives together? Couldn't they just have this time to be a couple before the baby came? She didn't want to be a hero and help save the world.

"Enough talk about this for the night. We don't have to find an answer now. There's time for you to pray about this and for us to pray together. Right now I want to enjoy the "wife of my youth" just like God commanded. We're going to be fine...All of us."

Noelle looked deep into the eyes of the man who was holding her tight. He was sending her a lifeline. He was letting her know this was not going to define them.

She kissed his face over and over. She loved the gentled curves and the permanent creases that were etched around his lips from his beautiful smile. The stress of the previous conversation tucked away for the time being. He was letting her know this wasn't going to consume them. God was in control. They were fine.

Chapter Six

Psalm 32:6

Therefore let everyone

who is godly pray to you

while you may be found,

surely when the mighty waters rise,

they will not reach him.

GENIE AND THE GIRLS HAD BEEN FORCED TO STOP their packing. They had gotten word from Brad and Noelle that they were coming into town to meet with the Prosecuting Attorney, Laura Lynn Lyndstrum. They weren't promising anything, just that they would talk with her.

Noelle seemed very unsure about all of this. Brad however was very confident they were headed in the right direction. He was sure God wasn't going to walk them into the fire without knowing they wouldn't get burned. He saw this as a huge opportunity of healing for Noelle. He shared the story of the silversmith who had to take the metal and heat it with such high heat to be able to bend and mold the silver into something beautiful and useful.

Brad understood many times during their lives together they would be called to walk through the fires of life. He also understood it was during those times that God was bending and molding them into who He wanted them to be. The fire would be purifying; burning out the unwanted areas. It wasn't the fire which would be the problem, it was the time they would spend resisting the molding. A completely surrendered heart would make for less time in the fire. He believed they simply needed to surrender to the molding quickly to avoid unnecessary time spent in the fire. He knew it wouldn't always be comfortable, but would always be beneficial.

It was this reasoning that caused him to contact the prosecuting attorney. He wanted God to see they were willing to be obedient from the very beginning. Brad felt this was his best way as Noelle's husband to protect her from the pain of this trial. He was willing to speed the process up so their time in the fire was less.

Genie was willing to trust in Brad's decision; yet she did so with trepidation. When he called to say they were coming, he shared this with her, "I feel like Noelle put a small band-aid on a huge sore. At some point the uncovered part of the sore will break open and start to bleed. The blood will leach into other parts of her life causing more harm. This is the time to fix the injury. I want to allow her to have time to heal before it continues to grow and hurts her more. This is going to be good. With God beside us, only good things can happen. *Jeremiah 29:11 For I know the plans I have for you," declares the LORD, "plans to prosper you and not to harm you, plans to give you a hope and a future."*

"I want to believe you're right Brad. But my mommy's heart is hurting for my girl." Genie wished she could be as confident as her new son-in-law. But the truth was...She wasn't.

This was a major challenge. She hadn't had enough time with the Lord to build her faith up to this point. She needed more learning. She wasn't sure she knew how to stand up against an enemy as big as this. Every day she fought against being bitter. Genie knew what happened when you didn't forgive. She didn't want to go back there again. It wasn't a good place to be. God had brought her out of that pit and she wanted to trust Him more. So she did the only thing she knew to do...She prayed.

God Almighty. Maker of heaven and earth. You knew about this day before You created us. Give us the strength to do what we have to do. Be with Noelle and Brad and protect them and their baby. I pray You will change the man who has done this to all of these young girls. Help him to find out who You are. Heal him from this sickness of the mind that allowed him to do what he did. Make a way for Noelle to heal without adding to her scars. You are a gracious God. I cry out for Your mercy. I love You. Amen.

Now Genie was trying not to take it back out of God's hands after she had given it to Him. Worrying wasn't going to fix anything. Only God could. So she prepared for Brad and Noelle. It looked like Noelle's old room was going to get used again after all. Genie hoped she liked the changes. She also hoped she wouldn't think it strange they had packed everything up. They were going to have to be sneaky if they were going to keep the secret.

Every day brought them closer to the moving day. Genie had been in contact with The Office of Public Affairs. The job sounded like something she would really enjoy. It appeared she would be in charge of the social activities around the campus. She would be the first line of connection between the University and the outside world media. The director of the office, Mr. Grady Yost, was a big man. A football player in his college days. She only knew that because she had googled his name and found out as much about him as she could. It was always nice to put a face to a voice. And a nice voice it was. He seemed gentle and sincere, yet energetic. She had already found out he was a Christian from the public organizations that he was associated with. She was thankful for that information. Now with her new life as a believer, she didn't want to have to feel like she had to tread carefully around the people she worked with every day. After agreeing on a start date for her, he had already begun sending her copies of the news releases the office put out on a daily basis. They were having conversation everyday and he seemed as anxious for her to begin as she was. The anticipation of a new adventure was making the thought of leaving her past more appealing. *Looking forward, I press on in Christ Jesus.* That was becoming her new life motto.

Genie would repeat that many times as she waited for her daughter's arrival. She was going to learn how to press on with the help of her son-in-law. Brad's daily strength was a good example for her and the girls. If he could do this fearlessly...So could they.

The young couple arrived late Thursday night and Genie could see the trip was wearing on her daughter. With an early morning appointment looming ahead of her, she ushered them off to bed saying, "We have all weekend. You rest for tonight." She kissed them off.

The girls weren't so understanding. They had missed their sister so much. But they knew the secret and that kept them going.

****

Attorney Lyndstrum welcomed them into her office right on time. Her job was to read people and she was good. What she was seeing was a young woman who wasn't sure about what she was doing. But the strength of her husband was evident. With a protective arm around his wife, Brad initiated the conversation.

"Mrs. Lyndstrum my wife is here because I think this is important for her to do for our future. She isn't eager at all to face her past. It was very traumatic for her. She chose to run from her problem. It was in the running that God brought us together. We married and are going to have a baby in July. I just want my wife to be able to deal with this demon so it can be put to rest forever.

94

"I see." The attorney turned to Noelle and asked, "Mrs. Conroy, is it okay if I ask you a few questions?"

"Yes." Her answer was tentative and unsure.

Laura Lynn knew she had to proceed with compassion to avoid further damage to the young woman sitting before her. "Am I to understand you are here to tell me you were raped?"

"That's right."

"How did you hear about this case?"

"My mom and sisters saw it in the newspaper and my mom works as Administrative Assistant to the Dean of Students at the University. I was a student there at the time of the...The rape."

"When was that?"

There was the dreaded question. "Friday night before last Halloween. I was at my first fraternity party. It was by invitation only. I was a freshman. It seemed like a big deal to be invited. Myself and two of my college friends were all invited. We went together."

"Did you leave together?"

"No. When I..." Noelle paused and swallowed hard attempting to stop the tears that were threatening to fall, "when I woke up the next morning, I was confused and groggy. I didn't know what happened to them. I didn't know how I had gotten into that bedroom or that bed. That wasn't something I would have done. I just knew I had to get out of there. I grabbed my clothes, putting them on as I ran back to my dorm room." Noelle didn't look up as she answered the question.

"What did you do when you got back to your own room?" The attorney pressed on.

"I got in the shower and I scrubbed. I scrubbed until I was raw. I couldn't get the feeling of filth off of me. I felt dirty. I felt violated. I felt...Raped."

"Did you tell anyone else?"

"No. I was so ashamed. I didn't want anyone to know. I didn't want people talking about me. I wanted to protect my sisters from all of that kind of ugliness."

Brad was rubbing her back in small circles. His reassurance was everything to her.

"Noelle, the baby you are carrying, is the baby a product of that rape?" It was a sensitive question; but Laura Lynn had to ask the question. She had to have this answer on record. The baby's DNA could seal up this case.

Noelle was silent for a long time. She didn't seem to be able to answer.

Brad said to her, "It's going to be okay Honey. God's here. He's holding us strong."

"Yes." She whispered the word ever so softly.

Laura Lynn soared. They had him. This baby would be the proof that pushed the case over the edge. She had to contain her excitement though. She could see Noelle was fragile and she didn't want to be here having this conversation.

Laura sat silently, giving Noelle time to regain her strength. She thought just for a moment about the words the young husband had used to reassure his wife. He said, "God's here." He insinuated that same God was holding them. Laura didn't understand any of that; however it did seem to give Noelle comfort and strength. The practiced attorney tucked it away and decided to mull it over at a later time.

"What did you do in the days that followed the rape Noelle?"

"I did life. I didn't want anyone to be suspicious. Then I found out that I was pregnant and I started making plans to run away. I just had to protect my mom and sisters. It's a long story. We had a bad year. My dad had left us. We didn't have any idea he was leaving. Up to the point he left, our life was wonderful. When he left, my mom, my sisters and myself, we were having a hard time adjusting. I didn't want them to have to deal with one more horrible thing."

Laura Lynn's heart was breaking for the young woman in front of her. She could feel the pain Noelle had lived through. This whole case was too close to her story to be comfortable. But this...A pregnancy that resulted from a rape...Brought her right back into her childhood. She of all people knew the stigma that can follow a child of rape. You don't really belong anywhere. No one wants you. You represent the bad moment in your mother's life and she can't love you. This was too similar to her childhood memories. She had fought hard to make something of her life. Maybe it was to prove to everyone she could. This case had stirred up a lot of ugly memories.

Laura knew that not all children in her situation lived the same terrible life. But in her wounds, she couldn't get past the pain.

"Mrs. Lyndstrum, God reached down and saved my life and the life of my unborn child. The last thing I want to do is get involved in a public trial. I don't even know what the man looked like that raped me. When I left that morning, his back was to me. I would just as soon not have to put a face to that memory. If you know what I mean?" Noelle's face was pleading.

"Why are you here Noelle?"

"Because Brad thinks God wants us to face this. Maybe there is a plan in action here. We're trying to remember God loves this lost son of His as much as He loves us. But, I don't want my baby involved in this mess and I don't want that man to think he has any right to this child."

"Noelle, I know how hard this is for you. I really do. Can I share with you that I am a product of rape. I carried the stigma of that through my growing up years. It wasn't until I went away to a college halfway across the United States, that I finally felt like I could shake the ugly off of my life. Without giving away too much of our case, I want you to know you are only one of many girls. This man has done a good job of ruining a lot of girls' lives. I want to see him put away. I want this madness stopped. You can help that happen. Now I can't make you any promises; but I will try to keep you out of the limelight as much as possible. Fair enough?"

"Yes. I don't want to see this continue either." Noelle said.

"How long will you be in town?" The attorney asked.

"Until Monday morning." Brad answered.

She handed Brad her business card and said, "Thank you."

Taking Noelle's hand into her own she said, "You are a brave girl. You're also one of the lucky ones. You survived and you will continue to live."

Noelle nodded. Standing, the attorney saw them to the door.

As it closed, Laura Lynn was already planning how she could use this information to put this guy away. She now had an ace in the hole. The passion from her past was rising up and being given an opportunity to find a victory over the injustice of the world. She wasn't going to let that get away. She would use this to the betterment of all of those involved. Including an avenue for her own healing. She couldn't go back in time and change what had happened to her and her mother; however, she could see that this one man could never hurt anyone else again.

****

A plan was developing in Laura Lynn's mind. Yelling out to her secretary she said, "Get me an appointment with Teo Mohan. Stat. Tell him I know something he's going to want to know." She was almost giddy at the thought. Then reeling her excitement back in, she was reminded of the woman, barely out of childhood, who had just left her office. This had been life changing for her. This young man, Brad, was certainly a gift. They were going to be just fine. She did have one concern though...

The Whitehall family has money. They have a lot of money. If they were to find out about this baby and that it was fathered by their son, what would they do? Laura Lynn wanted to make sure that didn't happen. She was going to have to think the next step of her plan through carefully.

Rebecca, her secretary, popped her head into her office, "Mr. Teo can see you for a lunch meeting. You have nothing on your calendar so I scheduled with him."

Laura Lynn didn't even look up from her computer as she typed up her notes from her conversation with the young couple that were going to be the nail that sealed her case. "That's fine. Just let me know what time and where."

Three hours later she was sitting at a local restaurant ordering a chef salad and drinking more coffee. Teo Mohan was sitting across from her and she could see him contemplating the conversation they were about to have.

"Okay. What do you have for me?" He asked. Very blunt and to the point.

"First, I want you to know we're getting ready to make a couple more arrests. There were guys who helped drug those girls. It doesn't look like they were involved in the rapes. It does appear that Mr. Whitehall bought their services with gifts and promises. We're going to charge them as accomplices.

"That doesn't really affect me." Teo waited. He knew they wouldn't be having this meeting if she wasn't bringing more than that to the table. It was the "more" he was concerned with.

"I have a girl who's pregnant with your man's child. Raped at a fraternity party on the Friday before Halloween."

"How do you know the baby is his?"

"She's as credible as they come. You and I both know that the baby's DNA will clinch this case. Your guy is going to swing."

Teo let her excitement ebb away. There was a sadness that filled him to know she was so happy to see a young man's life wasted. "So what are you offering?"

"I'm willing to give you twenty years in the state penitentiary; no parole and mandatory counseling. I also want him to sign away his parental rights. I'm not willing to negotiate. I want an answer within the week."

"Twenty years on a first offense? No way. Not without a trial." Teo sat back crossing his arms and looked firm.

"The trial is going to go in our favor. You've seen the reports. Everyday more girls come forward. I have a list of other instances he's been involved in that Daddy Whitehall made go away. His record is clean only because it's been bought. And...Need I mention...Judge Marshall isn't fond of your guy." She smiled knowing the last statement was a huge plus to her side.

"Don't underestimate my courtroom skills. I have a few tricks up my sleeves also. He smirked. "Here's what I will present to my client, 'ten years; time off for good behavior, we agree to counseling and he decides about the parental piece."

"Ten years isn't enough for all he's done. There are a multitude of girls whose lives have been tipped upside down." She was adamant.

"Listen. Don't get me wrong. The guy is a dirt bag. But he's what he was made into. Never had any rules. Lived a life of luxury. Always the big shot. Believe me, I get he doesn't have any social skills. Everyday of being locked up is killing him. Ten years will seem like a lifetime. But with some good counseling; he should be teachable. That's what I'm willing to present to him. What do you say?" Teo waited. He knew if he could get her to agree to the ten years, he had made the best deal for his client that could be made. If they started putting girls on the stand who were pregnant, this case was going down the drain fast.

"Here's what I say. He has two days and the ten years is pulled off the table and we're going all the way. As much as we can get. I believe this is someone who needs to be put away for as long as we can."

"Remember, our goal is to uniformly punish and then help to get them back into society as productive people. We should hope for them to serve their time and come out respectable adults." Teo felt the need to remind her.

He watched for her reaction. What concerned him was that he wasn't seeing anything. "Vengeance
101

is mine." Says the Lord. "There seems to be a little personal attitude coming through on this one. What's up Laura? I've worked with you for a lot of years. I've never seen you get this emotionally involved over a case." Teo's attitude changed and there was real concern for the person sitting across the table from him.

"Let's just say I understand some of the emotions that come from crimes like these."

"I'm sorry. I really am. We do a hard job. It's easy to become bitter. Don't go there. It isn't a pretty place and it clouds our perspective. You're too good to let that happen to you. Maybe you need a break. When's the last time you've had a vacation?" He smiled at her.

Softening just a little, "I don't even remember when I had a weekend off. It just seems like the good guys went on vacation and left all of the bad guys in charge."

"Really? What do you know about God?"

She looked like he had just dropped a bomb. Where had that just come from? This was the second time today that she had been surprised by talk of God. "I know He's never been there for me. Anything I got, I got on my own. I work in a world where He doesn't show His face. However, it's funny you should bring Him up."

"Why is that?"

"The young couple I talked with today, mingled Him in and out of their conversation all morning. They believe God brought them together through all of this travesty. The young girl's husband believes this is going to be healing for his wife. Strange, huh?"

"Not strange at all. He's a 'Big God'. You know there are two worlds at work here on this big, beautiful earth. The master of the dark side is just roaming around trying to destroy lives. God is capable of taking what

102

satan intends for evil and making good come out of it. There's always going to be a battle between good and evil until Jesus comes back and makes all things new." He was sitting there smiling like he knew a secret she didn't.

"Well...He better be a 'Big God' because it's going to take someone big to straighten out this mess."

"Come to church with me some Sunday. I'll show you how big He can be. It's a standing offer. Any time you want to take me up on it. I'll even spring for lunch afterwards."

She laughed, "We'll see. I'll have to think about that. I've never seen the whole God thing work. Always felt like I was on my own. We'll see."

"Fair enough. But let me throw this out. Forgiveness is a key element of God's kingdom. He forgave us our sins by sending His son to die on the cross for us. He expects us to forgive those who have hurt us in that same way. We can put a wedge between God and ourselves by being unforgiving. Don't get caught there. The young husband is really very smart and doing an admirable thing by helping her walk through this. Their lives will be better if she can find the freedom in forgiveness.

"I guess." Was Laura's only reply.

"So how did we end up with a husband involved in this scenario?" Teo asked.

"The young lady ran away to protect her family from the pain of the rape and pregnancy. She apparently ran into this young man. They ended up married. They really do seem very sweet together. I hope they have a happy ending to the ugly start."

Teo let the conversation move to lighter talk. He hoped Laura made the connection between her and the young couple. It was obvious to see she was stuck somewhere in her past. The hurts were still there, still fresh and still affecting her life. She had just covered them up and went on with life. Teo admired the young husband for recognizing the need for healing in his wife's life. He threw up a quick prayer asking God to bless them as they walked through this trial.

The two attorneys finished their lunch and went off to continue their daily schedules. But in the back of his mind, Teo was wondering just what made that lady prosecutor tick. Someone had hurt her bad. She wore her wounds almost like a medal. She apparently was a survivor in the war of life, yet at what cost. Too many casualties these days. Too many wounded souls. *God if I can help Your daughter, will You make a way?"*

Lunch over, Teo was going to have to make time to go over to the jail and talk with Delmyn. He wasn't looking forward to that conversation. Thinking to himself he wondered, *Maybe I should contact the parents' first. Delmyn has given me permission to discuss his case with them. They might have some suggestions on how to convince their son this was his best shot at making all of this go away.*

Walking back into his office, he asked his assistant to place a call to the Whitehall residence. "I would like to talk with Mr. Whitehall. See when he would be available."

The phone rang at Keefe Whitehall's office. His wife had given this number to the attorney's office. Answering, his secretary placed the attorney on hold and asked Mr. Whitehall if he had time for a call from a Mr. Mohan.

"Put him through please."

"Hello. Mr. Whitehall speaking."

"Yes Mr. Whitehall. Teo Mohan calling. Thank you for taking my call. I've just had a conversation with the Prosecuting Attorney Laura Lynn Lynstrom. She has put an offer on the table. I would like us to have some discussion. There is a time limit on the offer. Would it be possible for us to talk today? Mrs. Whitehall is welcome if you think that would be beneficial.

Keefe's stomach tightened. His immediate thought was this could not be good. "I can meet you anytime that works with your schedule. I'm not sure if we should bring my wife in at this time. She's very distraught. You can understand how this has upset her." He paused. "She loves her son Mr. Mohan...As do I."

"I'm sure this has been devastating for the both of you. I wish I could bring you better news. However, the circumstances don't offer us that option. Now we need to do whatever is the best thing for Delmyn. But let's not get into it on the phone. How about 4:00 p.m. at my office. I should be back from the Courthouse by then. Thank you for changing your day. I'll see you then."

Teo hung up the phone feeling compassion for the family. Even though he believed they were partly to blame for not raising their son with rules; he did understand their hearts must be breaking. Not being a father himself, he couldn't walk in their shoes. This he did know, being a parent is the hardest job anyone does. There's a lot riding on the decisions you make. You are molding an adult. One who's going to mimic your actions. That's just a ton of pressure. In Teo's practice, he had seen some good ones; but he had seen a lot of bad ones. He still believed God made the difference. Not religion. But a deep relationship with the Father who made us all.

He wasn't looking forward to this conversation with Delmyn's father any more than he was looking forward to talking with the son.

****

On the drive downtown to Mr. Mohan's office, Keefe's mind was running wild. He had hired a private investigator to do some checking on Teo Mohan. That wasn't what was working on his mind. Mr. Mohan's reputation was impeccable and his quality as legal representation preceded him. No...He wasn't the problem.

Keefe had also asked the investigator to do some checking on his son. His instruction to the hired man was, "See what you can come up with." The information was heart breaking. If this man could so quickly come up with all of the information he had, so could the police. He was beginning to understand his son was really in terrible trouble. He had created a mess of his life. It was a mess that wasn't going to go away. Keefe knew this meeting with Mr. Mohan wasn't going to bring anything that would make the situation they were in any better.

His son had done some terrible things. He wasn't even private about them.

Oh Del. How did this happen? Was it us? Did we love you too much? Keefe couldn't help the tears that were running down his cheeks. As a dad, he was feeling like he had completely let his son down. All he had ever wanted to do was love him and be loved by him.

****

A very somber Keefe Whitehall walked into

Teo's office. Teo knew this was a broken man. Here was a father who knew he was about to get the worst news possible. His attitude told Teo he wasn't going to be surprised.

Teo met him at the door extending his hand as he entered. Keefe took the hand knowing what this man was going to say would change their lives forever.

"I am sorry Mr. Whitehall."

"I'm just trying to figure out how all of this happened. How did everything get so out of control?"

Not wanting to assume he had any answers that would help him feel better Teo said, "I can't imagine how you and your wife are feeling. It has got to be some of the hardest pain a parent can experience. Please come in and sit down. Can I get you some coffee or tea?" Teo motioned him into a comfortable chair in a sitting area that seemed less threatening.

"No...No thank you. You have been most kind. I know I wasn't the most appreciative of your wisdom in some of these areas that I have found myself in recently."

"It's fine. These are certainly troubling times." Teo answered very graciously.

"Mr. Mohan, I hired a private investigator to do some checking. The things he brought to me about my son doesn't paint a very nice picture. It does paint a clear picture though. I just don't understand. I realize we were too lenient; but how did that translate into him becoming a monster? That's what my son is...He's a monster who doesn't seem to have any respect for anyone, including his parents. I promise you, his mother and I did not teach that kind of behavior. I don't even know how to tell all of this to Shauna. She is going to be destroyed."

"I'm sorry. I really am." Teo's compassion for the man sitting in front of him was too real for words to express. This certainly proves that money cannot buy everything. It cannot buy this kind of pain away.

"Mr. Whitehall, may I suggest sorrow like what you are experiencing is only able to be handled in one way and that's through a relationship with Jesus Christ. He is the only one who can understand and heal the brokenness you're feeling. I don't know where your family stands with God; but I can tell you I wouldn't know what to do without Him. Under the circumstances that Delmyn finds himself in, he could certainly use the love of Jesus." Teo paused giving him time to respond.

"You know, we never seemed to find time for all of that church stuff. I don't know...Maybe it would have been different for Del if we had made that more of a priority."

"It's not too late; not for you or for Del. Especially Del. He's going to need some help getting through this time. I'm afraid the same will be true for you and your wife."

Keefe just looked at him, lost, "I'm sorry Mr. Mohan. This isn't your problem. But thank you. Now... What do we need to do with my son?"

Teo shifted gears into a more business-like attitude. He wanted to make sure that Del's father grasped all that he was about to explain. "The Prosecuting Attorney's office has put an offer on the table of ten years with good behavior and mandatory counseling. We have two days to accept. Otherwise, they are moving forward looking for the maximum sentence. They will throw the book at him, as hard as they can. He could easily get double that sentence. They, too, have already seen the information your investigator has found."

"Ten years? How do they decide ahead of a trial that they can win?"

"Mr. Whitehall, there are girls coming forward every day. One of them is pregnant. The DNA of the baby will prove their case. This new information by itself will seal his sentence. When they discovered her, the original offer was 20 years. I negotiated the time in half. However, she would only agree to give us two days to take the offer."

"A baby. Oh no! My first grandchild was conceived in rape. Oh no! No. **No. NO.**" His head was spinning or was it the room. He went white as a sheet.

Teo got a glass of water and knelt down beside his chair. "Here drink this and breathe deep."

Keefe did as he was instructed. He didn't have any choice. There wasn't enough strength in him to do any differently.

Minutes went by. Teo could hear the ticking of the clock. Keefe could hear it too. It seemed like a roaring in his ears. Finally everything stopped moving and the moment of panic passed for Keefe.

"Help me Mr. Mohan. Tell me what to do."

"Our first move is to talk with Delmyn and get him to agree to the offer on the table. I would like your help to do that. I don't think he will accept that from me. He still thinks you're going to be able to get him out of this situation. My hope is I can get special permission for you to meet with us when I make the proposal. Are you willing to do that for your son?"

"I'll do whatever I can to help. If you think that is what we should do, I'll do it." Mr. Whitehall was definitely calmer and Teo could see he was starting to think all of this through.

"What about the pregnant girl? Is she okay?"

"I'm not at liberty to discuss any of that. I don't even know who she is. I won't know unless we end up

109

going to trial. Mr. Whitehall, we want to avoid that at all costs. It will not go in our favor." Teo was firm with his last statement. "It will not be in Delmyn's best interest."

Keefe stood up and walked to the window. "I need to think for just a minute."

"Okay. I'll be just outside the door." Teo wondered what turn they had just taken.

A few minutes went by and Keefe opened the door. "Let's talk again." He said.

Teo came back into the room and waited, giving the man in his office the lead in the conversation.

"I want to see the girl who is pregnant. I don't want anything from her. I just want to know she is okay. I want to apologize from our family. She is carrying my flesh and blood; a child that I may never know. I just have to see her." The look on his face said he was firm.

Teo proceeded cautiously, "I understand your concern. I'm not sure it is a good idea. Let's look at it from your side, we don't know the girl. Maybe she will find out how much money you have and demand assistance."

Keefe shook his head. "I hope she does. I would willingly give her money. In fact, I want her to take money to help with the raising of the child."

Teo could see this man was adamant and wasn't going to change his mind. "Let me talk with Attorney Lyndstrum. I assume that would only be possible if Delmyn agrees to the plea agreement."

Teo continued, "Mr. Whitehall you should also know that with the plea bargain offer comes a request for him to relinquish parental rights."

Keefe just stood looking at Teo. Walking towards the door, he turned and said, "I'll wait for you to call me. My cell phone will be on. I'll be available, whenever you make it all possible. Thank you. I know this wasn't an easy case for you. I am sorry." That being said, he walked out and closed the door.

Chapter Seven

Psalm 32:7

You are my hiding place;

You will protect me from trouble

and surround me with

songs of deliverance.

Selah

TEO HAD REALLY PULLED IN SOME FAVORS TO MAKE arrangements for Delmyn's father to be in the room when he met with Del. It wasn't the usual practice to allow a family member in for an unscheduled visitation. But it really wasn't a visitation.

He had also placed a call to Laura Lynn letting her know a request had been made by Mr. Whitehall to meet the young lady who was with child. She was "shocked at the audacity of the man". Those were her words. She continued with, "I will consider that conversation when you have accepted the plea." He wasn't surprised. It was pretty much what Teo had expected.

Mr. Whitehall was waiting on the front steps when Teo arrived at the County Jail.

"Thank you for being prompt." Teo said as he held the door open for them to pass through. Mr. Whitehall's comfort level told Teo he was not accustomed to being in this setting.

Immediately as they passed through the door, they were asked to empty their pockets into a small basket. The officer at the door, using a wand, checked them from head to toe. They were then allowed to pass through a metal detector and were given back the materials from their pockets. A different officer escorted the men to a room with windows. Teo knew they would be watched. It was part of being granted special permission. Teo could tell Mr. Whitehall also knew they were being watched. He didn't ask any questions. He was the epitome of professionalism. Again there was that feeling of compassion for the man waiting to face his son. The son who was facing this type of life for a long time; what would feel like a lifetime.

Delmyn was finally brought into the room and told to sit down. "Thank goodness Dad. I thought you were never going to get this straightened out. When can I get out of here? This is the worst place I've ever seen. They don't care about anyone."

To his credit, Delmyn's dad didn't respond.

Teo motioned toward a chair across the table from Delmyn and said, "Please have a seat Mr. Whitehall." Then looking at Delmyn he said, "We aren't here to take you out of here. You've been offered a plea bargain from the Prosecuting Attorney's office. That offer is only on the table for 48 hours and we're here to discuss it with you."

Delmyn looked back and forth between his dad and the attorney. You could tell he was confused.

"What do you mean you aren't here to take me out. That's what I want. I want to go home. Now!"

"Well that isn't going to happen. So I suggest you listen carefully to what they are offering."

Delmyn sat back in his chair and crossed his arms in a defiant position on his chest. "Okay. Speak."

The look on this young man's face made Teo want to vomit. Even in this situation he acted like a snot nosed little brat. Swallowing down his emotions he continued, "The State of Georgia is offering you ten years in the State Penitentiary with good behavior and mandatory counseling. As I said before, you have two days to accept their offer or we go to trial and they will throw everything at you. No more offers. You'll be facing the maximum penalties." Teo finished and waited for all of this to sink in.

"That's it. That's the best the two of you can do. Not acceptable. I'm not staying in here or anywhere

114

else. I'm going home. I'll take my chance in court."

"Your chance in court isn't worth a plugged nickel." Mr. Whitehall spoke up.

Delmyn looked at his dad with a look of total shock. "What are you talking about? Whose side are you on? We'll get another attorney. We'll get a better attorney who can do a better job. You just have to pay more money."

"No amount of money is going to buy you out of the mess you've gotten yourself into. Money can't fix what you've done." Keefe's voice was firm. His words conveyed a definite truth.

Teo watched the emotions play across his clients face. Del was shocked. It was easy to ascertain this was the first time his father had talked to him this way.

Keefe softened his words and his actions, "Son, there is nothing wrong with what Mr. Mohan has done to represent you. He isn't the problem. You...You son, are the problem. I hired a private investigator so I could defend you better; what I found wasn't going to help you at all. How did you get so far off track? Where did things go wrong? If I've done things that have hurt you, I'm sorry. All I ever wanted was for you to be happy."

"What are you talking about?" Del asked.

"I'm talking about the way you've been living your life. The things you've been doing. They are wrong. If I can find them, so can the prosecuting attorney's investigator. Who you've been, isn't going to help your case. In fact, it paints a picture of an irresponsible person who has no concern for anyone including himself. We didn't raise you to behave the way you have been living. Your mother and I are on your side. We always have been. We always will be. For your own good, I am telling you to take the plea bargain. That's the first step toward getting you some help." His father finished as he wiped the tears from his eyes.

"That's ridiculous. I haven't done anything wrong." Del really believed what he was saying.

"Those girls didn't deserve what you did to them. They have rights too. It was wrong."

"Dad? Those girls knew what they were there for. It's their own fault."

"Then why did you have to drug them? How can you think it's okay to bring someone to the point of not being able to defend themselves and then have your way with them? Were you that desperate?

"Those girls are fine. They were probably back at the next party. That's what they do."

"One of those girls is pregnant Del. She's going to have a baby. My grandchild."

"That's her fault. She didn't have to be pregnant. They have places to take care of stuff like that. If she needs money, just give her some."

Teo felt like he had been slapped in the face with that statement. He couldn't imagine how Del's father was feeling.

"Well Del, because of this attitude about life, you are going to be locked away for a long time. You can determine the time. You can either take the ten years and try to straighten your life out; or you can go to trial and get more time...A lot more time. Those are your choices. You choose. This time you're going to have to live with the consequences. If you choose to go to trial, you're on your own. I will continue to pay for your legal representation; because I feel a large part of who you are is due to my poor parenting skills. Just know, your mother will not be there. This is destroying her and I won't have her hearing all of the ugliness that is going to

116

come out about you and the way you were choosing to live. You are on your own this time."

"Dad you can't let them put me away. You have to do something." Del demanded.

"There is nothing I can do. I should have done my job better years ago. That is when I could have helped you. I didn't know. I would have done it differently if I would have known. You did this and now you're going to have to pay the consequences for your actions."

"Are you serious? You want me to be locked away?"

"Heavens no. But then I didn't want to find out all I did about the things you've done. You left me no choice. What's it going to be Son? Are you going to take your punishment like a man? The ten year offer is your best choice. It's going to be a lot worse if you go to trial."

"I can't do it Dad. I can't. You don't understand."

"I'm sorry Son. It's out of my hands. We'll try to get you some help. I'll see about getting you the best counseling that we can find. It will go easier on you if you take the ten years and try to work on coming out a better person."

Teo grabbed the moment, "Delmyn, we have to have an answer. We don't want this offer to be pulled off the table. I had to argue to get it reduced to the ten years. The jury will not go easy on you. You set the stage. Now the sentence is up to you. You can control this part of where you're at in life."

Truth was beginning to set in with Del. Realization was sinking into his soul. He wasn't going to get out. In fact, he was going to spend years locked up. Laying his head down on his hands he began to sob. Just like a little boy. His father came around the table and wrapped his arms around his shoulders. "You do this Son. We'll find a way to get through it. You need to stop fighting with everyone on the inside. You're only making it worse on yourself. Your mother and I love you. We don't want you to make this harder on yourself than it already is. Please Del...Accept the plea."

Delmyn raised his head and nodded okay. "How do I do this Dad? Tell me how."

"One day at a time Son and on the bad days minute by minute. The same way the girls you raped are getting by."

Wow. That was tough love. Teo gained a lot of respect for Mr. Whitehall in that moment.

Teo motioned for the officer on the other side of the door to step in.

The officer stepped in saying, "Your time is up."

"Thank you." Teo nodded to the officer. He wanted to get Delmyn out of the room before his dad broke down.

To Delmyn he said, "There will be one more courtroom appearance before the judge and then this part of the nightmare will be over. If I could make a recommendation to you, there is a jail pastor, his name is Pastor Preston, he's a very nice man. He'll help you through this if you let him. Talk to him. It'll help."

Del looked at him unable to speak.

Standing he turned to his dad. Taking a deep breath he struggled for the words, "I'm sorry. It wasn't you. I love you. Tell Mom I love her."

"We know. We love you too."

One final hug and the officer walked Del out the door and it closed shut.

Teo said, "Shall we go?"

Keefe just followed him out of the door.

118

On the steps of the jail, Keefe turned to Teo and offering his hand to the attorney said, "Thank you for everything. I will wait hoping to have an opportunity to meet with the girl."

Teo shaking Mr. Whitehall's hand answered, "I will do all that I can. Again...I can't promise you anything."

Keefe nodded letting Teo know that he understood. "How do I tell all of this to Shauna?"

"The Bible says the truth will set you free. It has always worked for me." Patting the shaking hand he said, "I'm sure we'll see each other again. I am sorry. I wish I could have done more." Turning, he walked away.

✶✶✶✶✶✶✶✶✶✶✶✶✶✶✶✶

As soon as Teo returned to his office, he phoned Laura Lynn Lyndstrum. It was after hours; but he knew she would be there. She answered on the first ring. "Why aren't you home?" Teo asked.

"The same reason you aren't. What's up?"

"I just met with Delmyn and his father. He has agreed to the plea bargain. Mr. Whitehall is still wanting to meet with the girl."

"I've been thinking about what that would look like. What is your feeling about a meeting?" She asked.

"I think part of it is to apologize and part of it is to see if she needs anything. I would say it might be very healing for both sides. Laura...There are two families destroyed here. Delmyn's family weren't monsters. They were parents who loved their kid too much and didn't teach him any boundaries. They're broken too."

"Okay. It seems pretty crazy to me; but I'll see

119

what I can do. If the girl says no, I won't push. Just so you know, she doesn't seem like someone who would want money."

"That's fair. Go home. It's been a long day."

"Thanks Teo." She hung up.

****

On Sunday evening after a wonderful day together, the door bell rang. Genie went to answer knowing that on the other side would stand the parents of the young man who had hurt her daughter. She didn't want to open the door. Her strength came from her daughter. If Noelle could do this, then so could she.

She hadn't been in favor of this meeting from the very beginning. What could they possibly say that could change anything now. Their son had raped her daughter. Instantly there was a check in her spirit.

Daughter, love as I first loved you. Show them who I am.

Genie knew what God expected from her. So she took a deep breath and opened the door. She saw instantly on the other side of her door stood two people who were equally as unsure about this meeting. The woman standing on the other side of the door seemed so frail that Genie's heart softened. For the first time she thought about what the young man's parents must be going through.

"Please, come in." She offered them her hand. "I'm Genie Smith. Welcome to my home. Won't you come and join us in the living room. The whole family is in there." She motioned for them to follow.

Silence filled the room as they entered. Brad, from the chair beside Noelle, stepped forward and shaking Mr. Whitehall's hand said, "Welcome. My name is Brad Conroy and this is my wife Noelle." He motioned toward her. She stood and walked towards the very sad looking couple.

"I'm sorry. This must be very difficult for you." Noelle acknowledged the brokenness she could see on both of the people standing in front of her.

"Yes it is; and also for you. Thank you for agreeing to meet us. You are more than gracious. I don't know what we could possibly say to make any of this better. Just...We are so sorry. Can you ever forgive us for what you have been through?" Mr. Whitehall shook his head. Shauna stood by her husband looking small and sad.

"Please come and sit down. Could we get you anything. We're all having some iced tea. Would you like a glass?" Noelle offered.

"That would be nice. Two please." Mr. Whitehall did all of the speaking. It was becoming very clear his wife wasn't handling any of this well.

After everyone was seated Noelle said, "Mr. Whitehall, Mrs. Whitehall, I have no reason to accept any apology from you. I hold no malice toward you. I've learned a lot during my walk with this challenge. I found a closer, more intimate relationship with my Savior. He carried me when I thought I couldn't go anymore. He brought me to a wonderful family, who showed me what God really looks like. They saved the life of my unborn child and in the end, God placed me into the hands of the man he created for me. None of that would have happened if I hadn't walked this road. I'm truly blessed; I've found peace and love. I'm in a good place. Surrounded by my family and the family God had waiting for me."

She continued, "I didn't know your son. But I hope you can all find a way to walk through this valley. I would recommend Jesus. He can make the dark days light."

Mr. Whitehall swallowed hard, "You are a remarkable young woman. I hope that someday my wife and I can find our joy again. Now the days seem so long. Delmyn was our only child. Maybe we loved him too much. The joy left with him."

"I know that feeling. But joy really can come in the morning when you trust in a Savior that loves us all equally, including your son. God's Word says it. I found it to be true."

"Can I ask you a question?" Mr. Whitehall hesitated.

"Certainly." Noelle answered.

"You said God brought you to a family that saved the life of your unborn child. What did you mean by that?"

"You see, I ran away from home. I was so desperate to protect my mom and sisters from the ugliness I was feeling. We'd had a rough year. My father, who we all loved very much, left us. Without notice. Just one day he was gone. We were struggling with trying to put our family back together again. I thought a pregnancy, especially the way this one happened, would just cause more pain. The only way I could see out of the mess was to go away and quietly have an abortion. God had a different plan. He dropped me right into the arms of a woman who had experienced the loss of a child. She showed me God and calmed the raging so I could hear His voice. In the end, Brad and I were married and we are anxiously waiting the arrival of our baby."

"I can see you are happy."

"I never thought I would get to experience the joy of this pregnancy. I didn't let myself think about the life of this baby. Without God, there is no end to the things you can consider. But with God, all things are possible. Brad's family showed me God and through His word, taught me how to hope again."

"This is our first grandchild; now, probably our only. This is a child we'll never know." The words were spoken so softly Noelle had to strain to understand what Mrs. Whitehall had said.

She answered with, "I'm sorry this has hurt you so much. I wish it could be different for you. I can see your pain. I do understand the crippling kind of pain that makes life seem so grim. I know you are wanting to be a part of this baby's life. I can't tell you I think that is a good idea. I don't know how that would affect him or her. How would I explain your presence without letting the child know he or she was conceived from a violent act of rape. That isn't something a child should be labeled with. Maybe down the road I would be able to see the situation differently. After I know my child and see the personality. There may come a day, when he or she is older, that I could see a reason to share this story with him or her. But not now."

"We understand. We really are trying to see this from your perspective. We would never want anything to hurt this sweet child." Shauna answered with tears slowly streaming down her very thin face.

"Do you think it would be possible for us to get pictures occasionally? Just an update to know the baby is healthy and doing well?" Mr. Whitehall asked.

"I think that it would be fine. If you would like to leave me with an address, I think I would be comfortable sending you an occasional picture."

123

Genie handed both of them a cool glass of iced tea asking, "Would you like sugar with your tea?"

"No thank you. This is quite fine."

The room was silent while they sipped their drinks.

Mr. Whitehall was the first to break the silence. "We certainly don't mean to offend you in any way; but we are very comfortable financially. Could we gift the baby some money? Are there any needs that we could meet for the two of you?"

"Thank you Mr. Whitehall. That's very kind of you to offer. We're comfortable and don't have many needs. God is our source and He is great at taking care of his people."

"We understand. We just want to do something to make up for what happened to you. It wasn't right. Our son was wrong to do what he did. Now he is going to pay a hard price for the ugliness he inflicted on too many people. We just want to fix it someway."

"I hold no ill feelings toward you or your son. I've had to work very hard at that. The Bible tells us *when we stand praying, if we hold anything against anyone, forgive him, so that our Father in Heaven may forgive us our sins.* I want to be forgiven. I'm just a sinner saved by grace. I want to keep an open door between me and my Father."

"I'll say it again you are a remarkable woman Noelle. My grandchild will be very lucky to have you as his or her mother." There was a long pause of silence. As if this couple, who were so uncomfortable, were hesitant to see this moment come to an end. Then he continued, "I think we've taken up enough of your time. Thank you for seeing us. We'll look forward to any pictures you are willing to share. If there is ever a time we could be of

124

help to you, please call. It would be our privilege."

Standing, they handed the glasses back to Genie and began to walk to the door.

Noelle followed them. Mr. Whitehall reached into his pocket and handed Noelle a business card. "Here is an address and phone number. You could reach us there."

Mrs. Whitehall, reaching her hand forward and looking to Noelle asked, "Would it be okay...May I?"

Noelle nodded.

Shauna placed both of her hands on the baby bump that protected the child inside of Noelle. "Bless you little one. May all of your days be filled with joy. We will love you forever."

There wasn't a dry eye in the house. Shauna turned into the arms of her husband and he lovingly helped her down the steps and into their car.

Brad came up behind Noelle and wrapping his arms around her whispered into her ear, "I agree...You ARE one remarkable woman and my baby is going to be blessed to have you as her mother."

Noelle turned into his arms and the tears flowed freely. Not because of the ugliness of the rape; but because of the unfairness of those that it affected.

Chapter Eight

Psalm 32:8

I will instruct you

and teach you in

the way you should go;

I will counsel you

and watch over you

IN THE MORNING, WHEN IT WAS TIME TO LEAVE, Noelle was surprised by the emotions that filled her spirit. She was going home and leaving the house that had always been her grounding point when she was growing up. In her heart, she knew it wasn't home any more. Her heart was where Brad was and now that would always be home. There was no sadness. Just a realization. Oh...She was going to miss her mom and the girls. This structure that had always meant so much to her, did not hold the same attachment. It was wood and brick. She would always have the memories tucked away in the recesses of her mind. Now her life had moved on and she was anxiously anticipating what was around the corner.

Standing at the door, holding onto her mom, Noelle said with tearing eyes, "I wish you were all coming with me. I want to put all of you into this car and take you back. I miss you so much when we're apart."

"I know Honey. We feel the same way. A piece of our hearts stay with you every time we say good-bye." Genie wanted to tell her there was a time coming when they would all be together and it would be soon. The agreement she had made with the girls, to keep the secret, seemed like a bad idea right now in this moment.

She could see the girls standing behind Noelle. Their eyes were full of tears; but they were giving her the look. "Stay strong. We can do this."

She couldn't spoil the surprise for them. So she said, "In a month you will be here for Nissa's graduation and shortly after that the baby will come and we'll be together. We can't wait to hold our little one."

"I know. The time is going so fast. There has certainly been a lot of life lived in this short time. I just wish we were closer." Noelle gave her mother a big squeeze and let go so she could hug the girls.

Genie stood watching her girls in their big, group hug. A peace about the move began to come over her. This was her family. The move was going to be okay. She could leave this house. It did not define her family. The love of people was more important. As long as she and her girls were together, her world was upright. With that revelation came the excitement of making the move. She hadn't really understood the girls enthusiasm to leave the house. Now she was realizing it wasn't about the leaving, it was about the going. They were venturing out into a new life, a fresh start. This was a good thing. Genie now couldn't wait to see what God had in store for her and her family.

The good-byes were said and Noelle and Brad were backing out of the driveway.

"Okay girls...Time for school. Get your stuff and I'll be in the car." Genie said as she grabbed her purse and opened the door.

"You almost told, Mom." Nissa accused.

"Yeah. I could see it in your face." Anaya chimed in.

"I know. I'm sorry. I just couldn't stand seeing one of my girls sad. Noelle was breaking my heart. However, I do think we should consider telling her when she is here for graduation. Maybe she'll need some time to say good-bye to her childhood home. This will be like closing a chapter in her book of life. Just think about it. We'll talk later. Right now you two stop stalling and get yourselves into the car." With that said, Genie walked out the door that led to the garage. Backing out

128

the car she threw up a quick prayer. *Father keep Brad and Noelle safe as they travel today. Angels around their vehicle. Help them to get safely home. Their vehicle unscathed by animals or other vehicles. I put them into Your hands. Thank you Father. Amen.*

The girls were arguing as they jumped into the car. Nissa couldn't find her black jacket. Anaya had apparently worn it and not given it back. Now it was buried in the mess of her room.

From the back Genie heard her middle daughter say, "Mom, I've been thinking about what you said about telling Noelle. I think it's true. I have been kind of saying good-bye as I'm packing. I felt like I needed to go and just sit at the swing set in the yard. I just wanted to sit there and think about all of the times we played back there. There were lots of memories to think about. I think I'd feel bad if I hadn't gotten the chance to walk down that memory lane. It was part of my packing up and shutting the suitcase on my childhood. Maybe we should tell Noelle."

"You girls have had lots of fun in the backyard. I want you to always remember those moments."

"For me it was the basement." Anaya said. "Last week I went down and played with the doll house. The three of us spent a lifetime pretending there. Nissa was always so bossy. She always thought she was the mom and could tell everyone what to do."

"Are you suggesting that as your mother, I'm bossy?" Genie pretended to be hurt by the remark.

"Oh Mom!" Both girls said in a sing song voice.

"All kidding aside, I don't think we should remove the option for Noelle to have her moment to say good-bye before the house belongs to someone else." Genie's voice held a sad note. "We all have our memories that need to be neatly tucked away so we can savor them for years. I brought you girls home from the hospital to this house."

"Mom, are you okay with this move? It happened so fast. I guess we never considered you might not want to move." Anaya asked.

"I'd be covering up the truth if I didn't tell you I've had my moments of sadness about leaving the home where I raised you girls. But, I've come to the conclusion you girls are right. For me it's the next move forward. To be honest with you, there was a part of me deep inside that was waiting for your dad to come back through our door. Here I can remain stuck in the memories. A fresh start for all of us is good. I think it was saying good-bye to Noelle today that sealed the decision for me. Now I'm ready." Genie smiled at Nissa in the front seat and checked the mirror so she could give Anaya a reassuring nod.

"I'm so proud you are my mom. Dad doesn't deserve you. That boat sailed and you're a beautiful woman looking for better fish in the sea." Nissa laughed at her own analogy.

"Nissa!" Genie was shocked to hear those words from her own daughter.

"What Mom? You ARE a beautiful woman and there ARE still plenty of good years in you. Some guy would get a real catch. Plus, we're all getting older. You aren't going to have as much to do in a few years. It's okay with me if you find another man and he makes you happy." Anaya jumped on the same wagon that Nissa had started rolling.

Genie was shaking her head as she pulled into the school parking lot. "You girls must be out of your mind. I can't even image opening myself up to someone else again. Now get out of this car before you're late for class." She playfully shooed them out the door blowing them kisses as they left..

She heard them both as the doors slammed saying, "Love you Mom!"

Pulling away, Genie wondered about the girls she loved so much. *Could they be serious? Would they really be okay if God brought another man into their world? Would she be okay with it? After all, it had hurt so much when Gale left. Could she ever trust someone again? And if not, what kind of a relationship would it be without trust.*

"Those are crazy thoughts." She said to herself as she began her drive to work. The talk of the morning had caused her mind to wander. There she was 20 years back, as if it was yesterday. She could almost feel Gale standing beside her in the front yard starring at the house. It was Gale's first big promotion and they had used the bonus money as a down payment. He grabbed her and began to run up the steps and into the entryway. "This is it Baby Girl. We are on our way up. There is no stopping us now. You and me. We've made it." She could feel him holding her hand. It was gentle and protective all at the same time. The laughter was flowing through her mind like a rippling river running and bouncing over rocks Laughing...Always laughing. They were happy; right up to the day that he left the letter and then the laughter died.

"Stop it!" She chastised herself. "This isn't helping any." She couldn't help but think maybe it was time for a new place; new memories; a new start. She was moving forward. No more roaming back through the "before". The memories too often took her to a place of sorrow about how much she had lost. She wondered,

131

if it would have been easier to have lived a sad life with bad memories instead of the joyful times that served to cause her pain when she visited.

Genie gave herself a good verbal shake and declared no more walking down memory lane. Her focus needed to be on happier thoughts. There was a new baby coming. Soon she would be learning a new occupation in a new town. Genie just kept thinking God must really have something wonderful in store for her and the girls. They had weathered the storm. In the turmoil of it, they had found that personal relationship with Him; they were learning to trust Him more everyday.

Philippians 4:19 And my God will meet all your needs according to His glorious riches in Christ Jesus.

And He was. Everyday there was more and more evidence of the love He had for Genie and her girls. "Thank you Jesus!" She was repeating as she pulled into the parking space designated for the "Administrative Assistant to the Dean of Students." He absolutely was good.

****

Preston was headed down Cell "C" again this morning wondering what his reception would be from Mr. Delmyn Whitehall. The last time he had been here he hadn't been received well. After the call he had answered yesterday, he hoped today would go better. It didn't happen often, but occasionally an attorney would call and ask him to stop in and check on one of their clients. So the call he received last night at home wasn't out of the ordinary. However, Preston could hear the battle in Teo Mohan's voice.

"Preston, this is a young man whose life has

changed drastically...And well it should have. He doesn't have a clue what to do now and he's going to be locked up for a long time. We all need Jesus; but this man needs a Savior desperately. He needs a lifeline. I have to be honest, he has pushed me to my limit of understanding. That's why I'm calling you. I'm hoping you'll be able to minister to him. Without Jesus, I don't know how he'll survive," Teo finished.

"I know the young man you're referring to. I've already stopped and introduced myself. To say that I wasn't received well is an understatement. I did get a Bible into his hands though. That's a start. I'll stop back in and see if he'll talk with me this time. Desperation is always a good motivator in my line of work. Thanks for the call, Teo. Hey...Tell me, how about you? Are you okay? I hear the fatigue in your voice." Preston waited anticipating the war weary reply.

"Sometimes it's hard. This case has especially tested my patience. It makes me wonder if I'm doing what God wants? Who am I really helping? Guys like this young man aren't really looking for help. They just want a free ride through life and they think they deserve it. I look at the parents and I think how did they become so clueless. This man was loved. Yet they gave him no rules. You know what happens in that situation? Chaos. Lawlessness. A life without boundaries is a life in turmoil. That's just where this family has landed; parents included. Now not only does the young man suffer; but his parents suffer also. Three lives destroyed. Not to mention the young ladies whose lives have been tipped upside down because of his selfishness. Sometimes I begin to wonder...Where is this world headed?" Preston could hear the exhaustion in Teo's words.

"To hell in a hand bag without Jesus. Teo you

need a vacation. Take a sabbatical. Spend sometime renewing your spirit before you can't help anyone. God created the world and then he rested. When was the last time you rested? I mean really rested. Go someplace and do nothing but soak up the beauty of God."

"It's been a long time and I know you're right. I can always tell when the pressure of this office becomes a burden. Right now I'm really feeling burdened." The sigh that Teo let slip out was a tell tale sign he was in need of a soaking break.

"Can I pray with you?" Preston asked.

"Absolutely Pastor. The more prayers the better," Teo said.

Father your son is weary from the battle. There are so many broken people out there who come across his path. Show your son favor. Give him victory in the war. Help him to make a difference in someone's life and make a way for him to find that sweet place of peace. He needs a spot where he can feel Your presence and know You are there with him. Even when he feels like he's walking through the valley of the shadow of death, he needs You. Take the burden of that earth curse from his shoulders and help him to be refreshed. Show him the foot prints in the sand where You are carrying him when the path feels too hard. Remind him "it is finished" and you have already been victorious over sin and death. Show him the purpose You created him for and help him not to grow weary doing Your work. In Jesus Name. Amen.

"Thank you Preston. I appreciate everything you do for these broken men and women. I'm sure you also get weary. I will continue to pray for your spirit and the work you do."

"You're welcome. And yes...I find myself weary

and in need. God knew what He was doing when He gave us the advice of a day of rest."

"We need you to take care of yourself. The work you do in the trenches is vital to changing lives. Good luck my friend. May God be with you."

✱✱✱✱✱✱✱✱✱✱✱✱✱✱✱✱✱

"Pastor Preston speaking" was his reply to the unidentified number that was causing his cellphone to ring way too early in the morning. The voice on the other end began to explain he had heard his name spoken by his son's attorney, Teo Mohan.

"My name is Keefe Whitehall and my son is incarcerated in the County Jail. He has just accepted a plea bargain that is going to keep him behind bars for a lot of years. Mr. Mohan directed my son to reach out to you. I am calling to personally ask you to spend some time with him. His mother and I are desperate. We need to know he is going to be able to survive. We were hoping you could help."

"And how about the two of you?" Preston asked. "How will you get through this trial?"

"We don't know. One day at a time we guess." Was Mr. Whitehall's reply. "I'm more worried about my wife. Everyday she's sinking deeper and deeper into depression. Del is our only son. We gave him everything, including all of us, apparently to his demise. We should have been stricter. There should have been more rules. We were creating a monster. We thought we were just loving him with everything in our power."

"Mr. Whitehall, without Jesus, each of us are capable of becoming a monster," Preston replied.

"I don't know much about any of that; however, I guess that could be true. Until now we hadn't really given religion a thought."

"I'm not talking about religion. I'm talking about a real personal relationship with the Savior who gave it all for each and everyone of us. Including you and your family." Preston continued. "Mr. Whitehall, I will definitely make it a priority to see your son and try to get him to spend some time with me. I actually have already stopped and seen him. I left him a Bible. I can't force him to open it up. However, I can tell you desperation is a great motivator and time isn't an issue for someone in your son's position. Time is all he has now. I can promise you if he will look inside he'll find a Savior who is just waiting to take the mess he made of his life and create hope. Jesus will help him build a new life. That life can surpass all he has seen so far. Regardless of where he resides."

Keefe answered, "I hope that's true. The life he's been living isn't a pretty one."

"There's nothing your son has done that can separate him from the love of the Father, if he'll only willingly surrender."

"That could be a problem. He doesn't seem willing to accept responsibility."

Preston could hear the hopelessness in the father's voice. "Well that's the first step. We all have to learn to surrender self and lay down our flesh. He'll have to recognize his past life of sin and repent. It's something we're all called to do. As sinners saved by grace, we all struggle with the human nature that has a propensity toward sin. That's why we needed a Savior. On our own we would never get to the Father." Preston hoped Mr. Whitehall was hearing all he was saying. His prayer was that these parents would not only see their son's need for a Savior; but also in their own lives.

136

Mr. Whitehall continued to unburden the grief that was holding him captive. "Pastor, my wife and I met with one of the young women and her family that my son...Well...Violated. She's pregnant. She's going to have my grandchild and I won't be a part of that child's life. She's real to us now. What a wonderful person. Not at all the kind of person my son describes these girls to be. She's forgiven my son for the terrible thing he did and she doesn't even hold it against us. I understand what you're saying about this Jesus. I saw His love exhibited through this amazing young woman and her family. There must be something to all of this. How else could she have forgiven the horrendous infringement my son brought into her life. If I would have only known, maybe we would have done things differently. Maybe Jesus would have helped Del."

"You can't go back, Mr. Whitehall. But you can go forward. Right now is always a great place to start. God doesn't hold us accountable for what we didn't know. He holds us accountable only for what we know and choose to ignore."

The conversation had been a hard start to his morning. It wasn't easy to hear the pain of a parent whose life was now changed because of sin. He had extended an invitation to the Whitehall family to join his family for Sunday morning services at their church. Preston really was praying they would take him up on his offer. Sometimes just an open hand in friendship was all that was needed to help someone take their first step. He had shared the conversation with his wife so she could pray in agreement with him for this family. "Let them see You Jesus, the Father who could heal their broken hearts."

Now Pastor Preston was standing outside of Cell

"C" where the broken young man burdening Teo and the Whitehall family was incarcerated. He waited for the door to slide open. Inside he could see the unmoving form of the man on his bunk. He threw up a quick prayer. *Father give me the words to reach this man. Prepare his heart to receive Your word. I'm asking for fertile soil. AMEN."*

The noise of the opening bars woke Del. He slowly rolled over and focused on the man standing inside his cell. His immediate thought was not a pleasant one. He had heard all he wanted from the man now standing in his small quarters. Something stopped him from saying what was running through his mind. Instead he thought about what his attorney had said about talking with this Pastor. Maybe he should try. One thing was for sure, he couldn't be more miserable than he already was.

"Good morning. Are you up for a chat today?" Preston waited for an invitation to continue.

"Why not. It's not like I got other options. Already had my 30 minutes outside." Del remained cocky and tried to appear in control. Preston knew better.

"So. How has it been going for you?" He hoped for an opening.

"Well...If spending the next ten years in lock up is appealing to you, then I would have to say everything's great." Del's sarcasm was burning through his words.

"So you've been sentenced?"

"Everything but the appearance before the judge. I took a plea bargain. My parents agreed with the attorney this was my best offer. Easy for all of them to say, they won't be sitting behind bars for a huge chunk of their lives. It's not their lives that are ruined."

"That's because they didn't do what you did." Preston wasn't going to let him get away with pushing

138

blame off on someone else. After all, his first step in repentance was accepting what he had done wrong.

"Yeah...Well...I didn't do anything so bad. Guys have been dominating women since the beginning of time."

"Is that what your dad does to your mom?" Preston asked a leading question and waited to see where it took the conversation.

"Don't bring them into this. My parents are great. They love me. They love each other. I had a great life." Del puffed up as if to emphasize how serious he was.

"So you love them too?"

"Yeah." He hung his head. Preston was glad to finally see some remorse in some part of the young man. "That's what makes this so bad. I know they're going to be pretty sad about all of this. I guess I really let them down." Preston was going to run with what he had been given.

"So your mom is pretty special to you then huh?"

"Yeah...She's the best."

"Well then, I want you to think about this for a minute. Those girls, the ones you drugged and violated, they were special to someone too. Someone loved them very much. Probably as much as you love your mom. How would you feel if someone did what you did to those girls; or what if they did that same thing to your mom?" Preston watched for reaction. This was the closest he had come to a telltale moment with the young man in front of him.

"My mom wouldn't have put herself in that situation. She's too much of a lady."

Preston was realizing how hard this guy was. He was going to be a hard nut to crack. He decided on complete honestly. He believed that honesty was always

139

the best policy. Even when it hurt.

"Well, I'll tell you what your dad told me this morning when he called to ask me to talk with you. He said he and your mom met one of the young ladies you raped. She's pregnant." Preston paused waiting for a reaction from Del.

"I know. She probably wants money."

"Wrong again. She doesn't want anything from you or your family. The meeting was initiated by your dad." He paused again giving all of this time to sink in.

"Here is the bottom line, your parents are struggling with the fact that this young lady is going to have their grandchild and they aren't going to know that child. You dad said, and I quote, 'she is an amazing young woman who has forgiven you for all you did.' They were even impressed with her family and the fact that even though you violated their daughter, they held no remorse towards you or them. You see, your parents, are carrying a lot of guilt for your actions. Not fair."

Del raised his voice, "What do you want me to do?"

"It isn't up to me to tell you what to do. That's your decision. Just like it was your choice to do what you did. We all have to live with the consequences to the choices that we make." Pastor paused giving Del time to think. "Unfortunately, your parents are having to live with the consequences of the choices you made too."

That seemed to touch a nerve. Preston could see the young man cringe.

"I can't fix it." Del said so quiet Preston had to strain to hear the words.

"The question is: do you want to carry the burden of your choices for the rest of your life?"

"What do you mean?"

140

Preston felt like he was just given a crack in the door, but he didn't want to throw the door open too wide. He wanted Delmyn to begin to dig for the answers. So he said, pointing to the Bible that was thrown on the floor beside his bed, "That book...It holds all the secrets to those kind of questions. I have to go, for today. I suggest you open it up and begin to read. The Bible is divided into two testaments, Old and New. Find the Book of John in the New Testament. It'll be the fourth book. Start reading there. You're a smart guy. See what you can find. We'll talk about it the next time I come by."

Turning toward the walkway, Preston waved for the officer to open the cell door. He decided not to even pray with the young man. The door slid open and he walked out. As he started to walk away he waved and said, "See you in a few days."

Walking out of the block he prayed, *Father grab a hold of Your son and fill him with a curiosity to search for You. Only You can change his life. I release this request into Your kingdom and thank You for all You are going to do. Amen.*

Chapter Nine

Psalm 32:9

Do not be like the horse or the mule,

which have no understanding

but must be controlled by bit and bridle

or they will not come to you

NOELLE AND BRAD HAD ENJOYED THE WEEKS OF settling into a routine. She would spend her days and some of the evenings at the restaurant. She loved learning from Angelina the ins and outs of the business. But mostly she loved greeting the people who came and for a brief moment in their day, she was able to wait on them and let them know they were special to her. Noelle understood completely why Angelina loved so much what she did. To many, the restaurant offered a rest stop along the way; a relaxing break in their day.

Quickly she had endeared herself to their regulars and soon realized this baby she was going to deliver was going to be the community baby. Everyone was eagerly anticipating the arrival of Baby Conroy. The funny part was that Brad had convinced them all the baby was going to be wearing pink. More times than she could count, in through the welcoming doors would come someone to eat carrying a beautiful gift for the baby. Almost always the present was for the feminine gender. It had become the town joke. Brad was having a girl. She had objected over and over; but always she heard the same thing. If Brad says it's a girl...Then it's a girl.

Noelle had decided to give over that battle. The baby would be what the baby would be. If pink was the wrong color when he arrived, then they would go and buy blue. It had become that simple in her mind.

So smiling she now just said, "thank you" and accepted the gift with love.

One thing she had learned through all of these weeks was the town had tremendous respect for her husband. The more time she spent as Mrs. Bradley

Conroy she understood why. Brad truly was a rock. He was patient and kind; and never a bad word to be said about anyone. His character spoke for itself. He was more trust-worthy than anyone she had ever known. And he loved her. When she thought about Brad, little goose bumps ran through her system. She couldn't wait to see him every day after work and she loved starting her morning with him at the house. Most mornings as she opened her eyes, there he would be, just watching her sleep.

One morning she opened her eyes and asked, "Why do you do that?"

Laughing he asked, "Do what?"

"Why do you just watch me sleep?"

Reaching over and drawing her into the crook of his arm, he gently kissed the top of her head. "You are the most beautiful woman I've ever seen. I'm still amazed every day how God brought us together. If I was able to sit and watch you day and night, I would never tire of doing just that."

Those were the words of love Noelle heard daily. She couldn't imagine life without him or the way he told her how special she was to him. Noelle planned on making sure he knew how much she loved him and how happy she was to be his wife. She was finding out that respecting him was easy; but loving him was even easier.

She thought about the times they had spent with Pastor Travis as they finished their marriage counseling that had to happen after the wedding. Pastor was doing his best of preparing them for the hard times that would come and Brad was telling Pastor they weren't going to live in that world. He would say, "Our marriage is created in the supernatural and that's natural in God's Kingdom. We don't have to live under those curses. We are living under His laws of blessings."

Pastor Travis would just laugh and say, "Who's teaching this class, you or me. I stand corrected. However it's important for you to know that God's word is clear, He calls you to love your wife Brad; Noelle you are called to respect your husband."

Noelle didn't always understand the things Brad was teaching her; but she was an eager learner. Many nights they would lay cuddled in bed and Brad would explain to her the laws of God's kingdom. Talking about how they weren't going to be living under the earth's curse. God was going to pour out His blessings on them because through Jesus Christ they were free from sin and death. He would say, "God's laws never change."

Philippians 4:19 And my God will meet all your needs according to His glorious riches in Christ Jesus.

"Our God owns it all and He created it for us." He would say.

Noelle couldn't be happier.

Tonight Brad had picked her up from the restaurant early. They needed to get their things packed to leave in the morning. Nissa was graduating and they were making the drive to Atlanta to be there for the ceremony. He wanted to make sure Noelle had a good nights sleep so she wouldn't be overtired. It was a long trip. Nine hours of good driving with no complications or slowed traffic. They were going to make a quick trip. He was planning on leaving at 7:00 a.m. and getting in on Thursday evening around 6:00 p.m. That would allow them a couple hours for stopping and letting Noelle stretch her legs while they grabbed a bite to eat. He was always thinking about her and Baby Girl's comfort. He didn't believe it could be good for their circulation to sit for long periods of time. His plan was to stop every couple of hours just to allow her time to walk around and stretch her legs.

With graduation on Friday and a party on Saturday, they would head back on Sunday. He didn't mind making the trip like that. He liked to drive. He was just concerned for Noelle and the baby. His plan was to do everything he could to keep them comfortable.

✵✵✵✵✵✵✵✵✵✵✵✵✵✵✵✵

Genie and the girls were watched as the clock hands moved ever so slowly. They knew Brad and Noelle were close; they had been on the phone with them regularly. They were anxious. It had been a month since they had seen her. Even though they received pictures regularly of her growing tummy; it wasn't the same as being able to put their hands on her and connect with the baby growing inside.

They were all in agreement they would tell Noelle and Brad as soon as they got there about the move. Noelle would have plenty of time to roam the house and find the closure she might need in saying good-bye. The girls were practically bursting with the announcement. They couldn't wait to let Noelle know they were going to all be together again.

Genie had gone into the kitchen to make the final arrangements for dinner when the girls yelled, "They're here! Off went her apron and she came running into the entryway. Nissa and Anaya were already on their way out to the car. Genie stood on the front porch and watched as her oldest daughter, still nimble, jumped down from the truck and into the arms of her waiting sisters. Her heart swelled watching the reunion of her girls. Seeing them together again just reaffirmed this move was looking better every day.

"Hey...What about me? Didn't anyone miss me?" Brad said and the girls turned into his waiting arms. Hugs for everyone.

Noelle saw her mom on the porch watching and started running up the walkway. Genie met her in the middle. Hugging her daughter felt so good. "I've missed this," she said.

"Me too Mom," Noelle answered back with a big squeeze.

Brad stood back and allowed mom and daughter the time they needed to share.

Looking up Genie opened an arm for her son-in-law to come into the embrace. He gently kissed the top of her head and said, "We've both missed you."

Her eyes got all teary. "Why is it you always make me cry? Come on in. I've got dinner made. We can catch up while we eat."

Through the laughter and food, Noelle quizzed the girls on everything she was missing about their days. The girls quizzed Noelle about the changes the baby was making to her body. What did it feel like when the baby moved? Did she slosh when she walked? Could Brad still put his arms around her?

"Girls! Genie lovingly scolded.

Brad fielded that one, "You won't see the day when I can't find a way to get her into my arms."

"Ohhhhh! That's the sweetest thing I've ever heard." Anaya said all gushy.

Nissa sighed, "I hope your brother is as romantic as you are. Otherwise when we get married I'm going to feel like I drew the short straw of the two of you."

This was the first time Brad and Noelle had been let in on her plans. They were on their honeymoon the last time she made her 'big' announcement. Suddenly all of the attention was on her.

"Is this something I don't know about?" Brad asked looking at Noelle.

"Don't look at me. I'm in the dark." She said.

Nissa continued, "I've made up my mind. Eyan and I are going to get married and move somewhere far away to work on a mission field together."

"I see. Does Eyan know about these plans?" Brad asked his sister-in-law.

"Not yet; but he will. God will let him know when it's time. I just have to be patient. The Bible says God will give me the desires of my heart. So I'm just going to love God more than anything so He can bless me with my desire. That would be Eyan. Just like God brought the two of you together, He'll let Eyan know about the plan in due time."

Noelle was marveling at the thought that her little sister could really be old enough to be thinking about marriage. Of course if she looked back less than a year, she would never have guessed then where she would be today. So who's to say it isn't possible. After all...**All things are possible with Christ.** Right?

"The mission field huh?" Leave it to Brad to focus on what everyone had missed.

"Yup. I don't even care where or how primitive. Although, I have been studying Spanish for 4 years and I recently began working with French. The two are a very similar language. Both could come in helpful in certain areas. It really doesn't matter to me. I trust Eyan to make that decision."

"Gotcha! Well Nissa, the mission field is an admirable direction for anyone's life. As for Eyan, we'll all just have to sit back and see where God takes that

148

one. He certainly didn't lead me astray when he brought Noelle into my life. I couldn't be happier." Brad finished.

"See...And it happened when you were least expecting it. God is going to nudge Eyan just like that. When he's not even looking, all of the sudden there I'll be. He's going to wonder why it took him so long." She answered in a very matter-of-fact manner.

"It would be easier if there wasn't so much distance between the two of you." Noelle mused.

"You are absolutely right, it would be easier. Wouldn't it Mom?" Nissa winked at her mother sitting at the head of the table very smugly.

"Why...Yes it would Nissa." Her mother answered. "Wouldn't that be easier Anaya?"

"Absolutely easier." Anaya giggled.

Noelle looked at Brad and then they both looked at Genie. "Why do I get the feeling that something is up and we're the only ones who don't know the secret?" Noelle questioned.

"Tell it Mom. Tell it!" The girls were cheering.

"Tell what?" Noelle asked again.

Genie took her sweet time and savored the news she was about to deliver. "Well, we were having a conversation with Angelina and Aunt Debbie before we left Indiana after the wedding about how nice it would be if we were all together again. After a brief conversation and prayer we were all in agreement that was exactly what we wanted. One thing led to another and within minutes we were on our way to look at a house just a few miles from Brad and Angelina's house." Genie allowed time for this to sink in.

"We met the nicest people. Professor Lee and his wife, Patty, own the home and they were just putting it on the market because they're going to be transferring to the University here. He was going to be looking for a house in this area. They came and stayed the weekend with us and fell in love with our house. We felt the same way about the home they have in Indiana. So...We are going to do a house swap. We're planning on moving next weekend. They want to be all settled by Memorial Day."

"What?" Brad and Noelle asked at the same time.

"You mean you are all moving to Indiana? We're going to be living close together?" Noelle was in shock.

"Yes!" Genie and the girls all answered at the same time.

"Why didn't you tell us?" Noelle asked.

Nissa took that one. "We wanted to surprise you after we moved there. But we got to thinking, maybe you would want some time to say good-bye to the house. You know, sentimental stuff."

"I can't believe it." Noelle was starting to cry. "I miss you guys so much and now we'll be together again. Oh my gosh...You'll be there when I have the baby."

The girls were talking all at once now. The excitement around the table was building. Everyone was laughing.

It was Brad who reeled everyone in when he said, "Look what God can do. You know what Nissa...Maybe you will marry Eyan."

And everyone laughed again.

✲✲✲✲✲✲✲✲✲✲✲✲✲✲✲✲

The band started to play "Pomp and Circumstance" which always made Genie cry. The graduates started down the aisle to take their place on the platform. A year

150

had gone by since she sat here watching Noelle do the same thing. She sat alone without Gale then and she was without him now. It was times like this she realized how much she missed their family. These were the times she had to fight the anger; to push back the question of why he wasn't here sharing the moment.

This year was going to be different. Her family was moving on and beside her they sat; Anaya, Noelle and her husband. She treasured watching the love between them, the bond they had created. Brad's love was evident in the attentive way he protected all of them. His display of affection for all of them was clear even as he and Noelle held hands and shared the excitement. In less than 60 days they would be welcoming a beautiful new baby into their lives. The bounty of God's blessings full and rich.

Would this have been the life direction Genie would have chosen? No. She would have wanted Gale to share all of this with her. But her family had defined a new normal. They were now survivors. This year they had learned they could do anything as long as they were together as a family. Next weekend would complete the circle once again. They would all come together. Genie couldn't wait. She was actually beginning to eagerly anticipate the move. Time really does fix all things.

Genie's sister Debbie snuck in right behind the graduates. She had gotten there just in time. The family squeezed in a little closer to make room for her. Hugs for the newlyweds as Genie relaxed and enjoyed the ceremony. Nissa had earned the right to share this moment with her family and Genie realized, looking down the row of bleachers at those she loved, that was just what was happening. Her family was beginning to feel complete again after a long period of what appeared

151

to be brokenness.

After the ceremony and a moment for pictures, they all loaded up and headed to a local restaurant for dinner. Funny how Noelle watched every move that was happening around her. Constantly comparing what was done here to what happened in her restaurant. She laughed at the realization of possession she felt for the restaurant. But it was true. She felt very much at home there. As if another piece of her life puzzle was being put into place. She would have never guessed she could have loved the work so much. However, Angelina had put a different twist on restaurant work. She taught her how to see it as a mission field, making the work so much more gratifying.

The talk was all about the party tomorrow. They had decided to have it at the house. A tent had been delivered and set up today and tomorrow morning the caterers would be arriving with the food. Picture books of a review of Nissa's life had already been put together. It was fun to walk back through her years and see how she had blossomed into a young woman. Brad was especially enjoying the life review of the family he loved. He knew God must be proud and Brad was certainly feeling blessed to have all of them in his life.

Everyone tucked in early after the busy day of celebration. Tomorrow would be a repeat of the same. People in and people out. Explanations about their move. Introductions and questions about Noelle and Brad. For many, tomorrow would be the first they would be told about the wedding and the baby. Genie wondered what kind of questions there would be. Would people be rude enough to ask questions that were purely for gossip. After all, these were the people who were supposed to care about them. They would also be the people who had talked the most about them when Gale left.

Oh well. Let tomorrow bring what it brings.
Genie thought to herself as she slipped off to a peaceful
sleep.

****

The day was beautiful. The sun came up bright
and early. It was going to be the perfect day for an outside
reception. Everybody was prepared and ready as the first
guest arrived. What took them by surprise happened
towards the end of the day. People were starting to leave
and the caterers had begun the process of putting away
the food when a delivery truck pulled into the front drive.

Genie happened to see it pull in and knew it
would be for Nissa so she went into the back yard to get
her. She told her there was a special delivery at the front
door and Nissa was followed by the rest of the family to
see what it was.

Signing for the delivery, Nissa unwrapped the
package of an exquisite bouquet of flowers. With an
envelope attached to it. Nissa opened it up and shock
covered her face.

Handing the letter to Brad she asked, "Will you
read this. I can't."

Brad took the letter and looked at the signature.
"Do you want me to read it out loud to everyone?"

"Yes, please." Nissa answered.

Genie's heart was barely beating. She knew who
had sent the letter and she didn't know if she could listen.

Brad looked at Noelle and she stepped over to
her mother's side and took her hand. She nodded for him
to start.

"To my beautiful daughter Nissa. I know this

must come as a shock for you to receive this from me; but I couldn't miss one more of the milestones in the lives of my girls. You have all grown into such beautiful women. You all look so much like your mother. When Noelle graduated, I couldn't bring myself to send anything and it broke my heart. I wanted so bad to see her walk down that aisle. I would have been so proud. The timing was all wrong. So I missed it. I know it was my own fault. I put no blame on anyone but myself. However, I couldn't do that again. I was there. I saw you receive your diploma and I couldn't have been prouder. Regardless of the things I have done in my life that I am not proud of, know you girls are the best thing I've ever done or ever will do. I wish I could be stronger. I wish I could hold you and give you kisses. I wish things could be different. Not a day goes by that I don't think about the three of you and know what I have lost. I'm sorry for the pain I've put your mother and all of you through. I ask God to find a way for you to forgive me every day. Please, celebrate the good we shared. Help me to hang onto the memories of yesterday. I cherish those thoughts and I live there continually. All of my love, Dad.

You could have heard a pin drop. The silence was almost deafening. Brad looked to the faces of the women he had come to love. Each had tears slowly falling down their cheeks. No one moved. It was as if they didn't want the moment to pass. They wanted to hang onto whatever it was they were feeling. So they stood for what seemed an eternity.

It was Nissa who finally broke the silence. "Wow."

"Right." Anaya said.

Noelle looked at her mom. She looked like she had seen a ghost.

154

"Mom...Are you okay?" Noelle wrapped her arm around her mom's shoulder so she could share the strength she had found in forgiveness.

"I will be." She answered.

Taking a deep breath Genie said, "Nissa, that was very nice of him. I'm sure he is very proud of you...Of all of you girls. He always loved you very much. Is there an address where you can send a thank you?"

Brad answered after checking over the envelope, "No there's nothing but a gift of cash."

Anaya finally spoke up, "Are you serious? He thinks he can just send a bunch of flowers and money with a ridiculous note and that's going to make it all better. Well, I'm not buying into this. He took a hike and I would just as soon let him keep on walking.

"Anaya. Haven't we been working on forgiving him? Regardless of what he does, we are still called to forgive." Nissa said to her sister.

"Well I'm just saying it was easier to work on forgiving him when I didn't know anything about him. I'm not there yet. I don't want to hear how he misses us. We haven't gone anywhere. He knew where we lived. It's his shame he needs to deal with. I don't have any. I didn't do anything wrong. I'm going to my room. I'm tired. Call me if you need any help." And with that Anaya left the group.

Noelle started to follow her little sister and Brad stopped her. "Why don't you give her a few minutes to process all that's just happened. Maybe in a little while she could use a talk from her older sister." Noelle looked into the loving eyes of her husband and decided to heed his advice.

Genie, deciding she needed to follow up in the backyard, left the group. Debbie followed her. Leaving only Brad, Noelle and Nissa standing there with the bouquet of flowers.

"What do you guys think?" Nissa asked.

Noelle just shrugged her shoulders.

"Brad?" Nissa continued, seeking.

"Well...Reading through this letter, I feel like your dad has paid a big price for the decision he made. I can't image the pain he must live with every day. It must be hard for him to look at himself in the mirror. I'm sure he isn't the person he wanted to become. God isn't going to let him rest until all of this pain has been put to rest. I would say he's a tortured man." Brad stepped over and took both girls into his arms. "I'm sorry this is hurting all of you. I wish I could make it all better."

"Thanks Brad. Your opinion matters to me. I think I'll go to my room too." Nissa took the flowers and the letter and headed up the stairs.

"I think he sounds sad, too." She said as she turned and left.

Noelle snuggled into her husband's arms where she felt so safe and protected. "I want to be mad at him for my mother; but I agree with Nissa. I think he did sound so sad."

"Nobody would fall into sin if they considered how miserable they were going to feel in the end." Brad kissed her forehead. "Let's go and see if we can help with anything in the backyard. Unless you need to lay down?"

Nope. I'm good. I'm sure mom can find something for us to do."

"If she can't...I can always think of a few things to do with you." Brad smirked.

Playfully Noelle bumped his arm; but that didn't change the look in the eyes of her husband. She hoped

156

that look never left his eyes.
"I just bet you can.".

Chapter Ten

Psalm 32:10

Many are the woes of the wicked,

but the LORD'S unfailing love

surrounds the man who trusts in him.

MEMORIAL DAY DAWNED WITH THE FEEL OF NEW beginnings. They were in. The swap had been made. Professor Lee and Patty were content in their new abode and the delivery truck had arrived with Genie's and the girls' belongings yesterday. The big furniture had been put into position, at least for now. The boxes were deposited into their respected rooms according to their labels. Now the challenge of unpacking and deciding what to do with everything began. Genie only had seven days to get everything in some semblance of order before she was to start her new job.

She had been in continual contact with her new boss, Grady Yost. She was becoming more and more excited about her new duties. It looked like the new job was going to be exciting and as fulfilling as the position she had just left; but in a different way. When working with Michael, she had more hands-on contact with the students. She had loved that part of her job. This new position was more news oriented. She would be working with TV, radio, and newspapers. There would be activities to plan; meetings to host; fund raisers to organize. She couldn't wait until next Monday. But for now she had work to do and so did the girls.

As she unpacked, she was thinking back on the last day at her home. Leaving was harder since the letter from Gale. That letter opened up wounds that had begun to heal. Crazy thoughts began to go through her head like what if Gale wanted to find them. He wouldn't know where they had gone. What was she thinking? What difference did it make? She didn't know where he had gone either. That was the way he had wanted it. Remember that Genie?

So, here she was working on healing those opened up sores again. When would this problem go away?

✱✱✱✱✱✱✱✱✱✱✱✱✱✱✱✱✱

Getting her mom and sisters settled in their new home was so exciting for Noelle. She was glad they had told her while she was home about the move. That last trip home for graduation gave her the opportunity to walk through the house and yard with Brad and tell him wonderful stories about their growing up. She shared the good and the bad. It was a time for closure. Brad helped her to look back and appreciate the past as he shared the beauty of their future.

Now was the time for new beginnings and new birth. The month of June was going to be all about getting ready for the baby.

For Angelina and Genie, becoming Grandmas was almost as exciting as having their own children. Maybe more. However, they agreed they were more concerned about Noelle having the baby than they ever were about delivering their own. The two women had become very close. Most Saturdays they would find sometime to take a little shopping trip looking for just the right item for the nursery. Sometimes Genie would buy something she thought she needed to have at her house when the baby would come to visit.

Noelle and Brad would lay in bed and laugh at the eccentric behavior of their two sensible mothers. Yet they loved every minute.

By the end of June everything was ready. Baby was already getting into position. Noelle's body was getting itself ready to deliver. The doctor was cautiously preparing them to be ready for an early birth. First babies usually take longer to arrive; but this baby looks like it's getting anxious. She warned them about not taking any lengthy trips.

Angelina tried to insist that Noelle stop working at the restaurant. It was to no avail.

"What would I do with myself? I can't just sit around and rock. No...I want to work. If it gets to be too hard, I'll reconsider. Besides, I can always sit if I feel that's necessary," Noelle was adamant.

Angelina tried to enlist Brad's assistance in the matter. He just laughed at her. "No one ever told my mommy cows to take a break. This is a natural process. Noelle is healthy and happy. She's fine. I know. I'm watching too. I won't let anything happen to her. Relax, momma hen!"

"Oh! Sometimes men are so exasperating!" Angelina said as she marched away from her still laughing son.

****

Back in Atlanta Pastor Preston was headed into a study at the jail. He was remembering back to the angry young man he had met that first visit in Delmyn Whitehall's cell. Preston had given Mr. Whitehall a little reflection after their second meeting. When he entered his cell the next time, there was a difference in the young man. He was full of questions and eager to learn more. In fact it wasn't long before he was asking Preston to pray the sinner's prayer with him. Jail house conversions were common. What better things did they have to look forward to besides reading the Word of

God. Not that Preston took it lightly. He didn't. A lost soul coming to Christ was always a beautiful moment. The problem comes when they go back home and have to face everyday life. With Del, unfortunately there was going to be a lot of time for him to fill up his God tank.

Pastor Preston didn't know how much time Del had before he would be transferred to the State Prison. He hoped he would have enough time to teach him how to get the most out of the Word. He wanted to have plenty of prayer time with him. He had already gotten him plugged into all of the Bible Studies that were going on in the jail. Every opportunity to learn more was good.

Today when he met him at the Bible Study he had to say he wasn't expecting the questions he was asked.

"Pastor, I know this may not be possible; but I've been thinking I would like to apologize to the girls I hurt. Do you think there would be anyway for me to do that?" Preston could see that Del was sincere.

"You know, I just want to say I'm sorry. Especially to the girl that's pregnant. I've been thinking about the baby. I know from my dad that she's married. You know I really didn't have anything to do with that pregnancy except depositing my sperm. That sure doesn't make me a dad. I hope she isn't planning on telling the kid I was ever in the picture. I mean...I wouldn't want the kid to think he came out of something as ugly as what I did. You know a kid should just get to be a kid. I don't want to add to the list of lives I've screwed up."

Preston was thanking God as he listened to this new Delmyn talk. With Christ old things are passed away and all things are made new. Including Delmyn Whitehall. "I don't know if it's possible. I would guess that the person you should talk to is Teo Mohan. Maybe he would have some suggestions."

162

"Yeah. That probably is a good place to start. I really need to apologize to him too. I didn't show him my best side when all of this started."

Preston laughed, "When all of this started, you didn't have a best side. That's why you needed Christ."

Del took his comment with good nature. They had developed that kind of a relationship. Del felt like he could call him friend. "Hey you know I probably owe you an 'I'm sorry' also. And a thanks for sticking around long enough to help me find some peace in my life."

"You're welcome."

"You know, you probably saved my mom's life by getting them plugged into a church. She was headed down a bad road with me. She has always struggled with depression. Probably having me for a son didn't help. I certainly had my moments. She spent so much time trying to please me that she lost herself in the mix. When we talk now she seems to be doing better. Not that she's ever happy to see me in here. But she's in a Bible Study with a group of women that really seem to care about her. It helps. Thanks for that too."

"Wow...You're really on a roll today." Preston patted him on the back as he prepared to leave. "You're going to be okay Mr. Whitehall. God's still got a plan for you."

With that said, Preston gathered the group of guys who had come together to study about the God who loves them more than they had ever understood. It was a good group. He was always amazed at the depth of the men in these groups. They came from all walks of life. The majority of them came from hardship and struggle. The choices they made brought them to this place. But through their brokenness, God found them and they cried out to Him, accepting Him as their Lord and Savior. Without coming to this place, many of them would have never found the God of love. Preston's hope was always that they would be strong enough when they left to take their God and share Him with family and friends. He always prayed for their words to be received and lives to be changed.

The solitude of jail life can bring you to a point where God can make His voice heard. Without it, some of these men would have never quieted the chaos in their lives, so they could find Him. Take Paul as an example. Paul was slowed so many times in prisons that the majority of the New Testament was authored by him. God will use every opportunity we find ourselves in to His good if we will just allow that to happen.

The next morning Del asked to place a call to his attorney. Teo's secretary transferred the call.

"This is Teo Mohan. How can I help you?"

"Mr. Mohan, Delmyn Whitehall speaking. Before you hang up on me, I want to tell you I'm sorry for all of the trouble I caused you. Thanks for hanging in there with me and for being real. You gave me truth when I needed it most and wanted it least. Without you I would have really messed things up more than I did. You were right about Pastor Preston. He's been a huge help to me and my parents. I've given my life to the Lord and my parents have plugged themselves into a church where they're getting help learning how to cope. I wish it didn't have to be this way; but better this than a life without Jesus. Right?"

Teo was speechless. He really didn't know what to say to the young man on the other end of the phone call. "Well Delmyn, I accept your apology and I'm thrilled to hear you've found the Lord. He'll make your life better no matter where you are."

"I know. I've really been feeling convicted about a lot of things in my life. That's another reason I needed to call you. Mr. Mohan, sir, I'm feeling like I need to somehow apologize to all of the girls I hurt. Especially the girl that ended up pregnant. I don't know how to do that, but I was wondering if you could help me figure it out?"

Teo was totally speechless again. He was even more convinced than ever that he was talking with a changed man. But as far as having conversations with the girls, Teo wasn't sure how he could help. Then he thought about Laura Lynn Lyndstrum. He wondered if she could help in some way.

"Delmyn I think that is very admirable of you and I understand your heart in wanting to do this. Why don't you let me do some checking and see if there is anything that can be done. Give me a few days and I promise I'll get back with you. I'm not making any promises. I don't know we can make this happen. I'm just promising to do some checking. Okay?"

"Okay. And thanks for anything you can do. It really is important to me. I owe them that much. You know where to find me. I'm probably going to be here for a few more weeks."

"I'll do my best. Thank you Delmyn. I'll be in touch."

With that, the connection was broken and Teo sat in his chair in amazement. The young man at the other end of the line was certainly different than the one that had caused him so much grief. All he could do was pray. *Thank you Jesus for Your faithfulness in this young man's life. And thank you for letting me see the change in him. I was getting so discouraged with the job you have me in. Help keep Del on the right path. Give him extra strength when satan tries to stop his journey towards You. Be with his parents. Give them Your peace. Continue to walk with all of us. Without You life would be too hard. Amen.*

Teo made it a point to call Laura Lynn right after he got off the phone. "Good morning. I'm glad I caught you. Have lunch with me? I have a question to ask you."

"About what?" She asked.

"I'll talk to you when we meet."

"I don't know. I have a crazy afternoon going already. I really don't have time for lunch."

"Oh come on. You have to eat, so how about I'll pick us up something and we'll meet down by the river on the board walk. We can at least have a little conversation while we're having a quick bite." He'd given her all of the charm he could muster at the spur of the moment.

"All right." She with an exasperated tone. "What time?"

"You tell me."

"I'll meet you at 12:00 sharp. Don't be late and I only have a few minutes to spare. Don't drag this out. See you then." She hung up.

Teo was left staring at the phone in his hand. "And...Good-bye to you too." He said to no one on the other end of the line. "I hope Mr. Whitehall appreciates what I'm about to do. I could be setting myself up for a thrashing." He chuckled to himself as he again prayed, *"I could use a little help with this one Father."*

The sun was warm on his face as he hurried with the brown bag lunches from the downtown deli. Chicken salad on whole wheat with a dill pickle and chips. He wasn't sure what Ms. Lyndstrum would want to drink; so he grabbed both pop and water. She could have her pick. He didn't really care.

He got to the bench just in time to see Laura Lynn get out of her car. She spotted him and walked briskly over to where he was sitting.

"This had better be good," was her first comment.

Handing her the sack lunch he said, "I hope you like chicken salad."

"Thank you. It's fine."

He held up both bottles of drink and she took the water leaving him with the pop.

"So what's up?" She jumped in not waiting for him to initiate the conversation.

"Mr. Delmyn Whitehall, the young man from the rape case, contacted my office today. He's been meeting with Pastor Preston. I was very impressed with the change I heard from the other end of the conversation. He called to apologize for all the problems he had caused me." He paused.

She jumped in, "Jail house conversion. I don't buy into it. You know what they say, 'There aren't any atheists in a fox hole'. Same difference. What more does he have to do than read what he's given. I've seen all of that before. The question is, if he was free tomorrow, what would his life look like? The old or the new man. That's really the only way you'd know." She finished as she continued to eat her lunch.

Teo was a little taken back by her cynicism. This wasn't going to be easy. But...He was jumping in with both feet.

"Well...He seemed very sincere. This is the question. He would like to apologize to the girls he

167

'hurt' was the way he put it. It seems very important to him to be able to tell them...."

Before he could continue she said angrily, "Are you kidding me? Are you serious? You think I'm going to give him those girls' names so he can harass them? Not for your life would I do that!"

He could see she was adamant. "He didn't ask for their names or addresses. He just wants to know if there is some way he could apologize. I think it's part of his healing process. And for all you know, it might help the girls heal too."

"Those girls don't want to hear from him. It's too late."

"That isn't a very forgiving spirit. Are you answering for them or is that your feelings?"

Ouch! By the look on her face, he wondered if he had pushed that one a little harder than he should have.

She looked at him, about to give him both barrels, then stopped. She changed her demeanor. "Maybe it was my thoughts." She paused a moment, then continued. "Here is what I'm willing to do. You have your client put together his apology letters and I will read them. If they pass my inspection and if I think they will help the girls and not cause them more grief, then I will pass them on. But you make sure he understands if I don't like the flavor of the apology...They are trash. Got it?'"

He saluted her, "Yup! I got it."

Teo decided as long as he had gone this far, he might as well keep going, "Why are you so hard?"

"You think this is hard, you should see me in the courtroom." She answered with a look that left no doubt in his mind.

He was sure she could be brutal without looking back. "You're a pretty woman, ever feel the need to show that feminine side?"

"Why are you asking?"

"I don't know...Just curious."

"My job doesn't leave me much time to worry about any other side. This has been my life ever since I left law school. Being a woman makes it tougher. You can't let your guard down or someone is trying to take what you've earned. Might be unfair; but that's the arena I play in."

"There's more to life than what you do. That should be your job and then outside of there is your real life. Come to church with me? The offer is still on the table." He threw her a sideways look that to anyone else would have seemed endearing.

"If I didn't know better I'd say you were making a pass at me." Laura chided.

"A pass...I asked a friend, if I can refer to you in that manner, to church. That's all. Plus, if I recall, I promised you lunch afterwards. All you have to do is say yes. You might find that you like it."

"Oh, I know all about church. I've seen the 'holier than thou' people who think they have all of the answers. I grew up in the midst of them."

"Sounds like you had a bad experience." Teo pushed on hoping she would open up and let him have a glimpse into what made her tick. For some reason, she fascinated him.

"You could say that." Was all that she was going to give.

"Not every church is the same. Just like not all people are the same."

"Really. Well you know the old adage that says, 'Fool me once shame on you, fool me twice shame on me', I'm not looking to set myself up for a second go round."

"Who are you really Laura Lynn Lyndstrum?" He asked sincerely.

"Who cares?" She answered.

"I do."

She could see the compassion in his eyes and for whatever reason she didn't understand herself she began to tell him. "I was a product of rape. My mother was raped by one of the righteous men of the local church. He was a family man. I grew up with some of his kids. We didn't play together. I wasn't good enough. I didn't know why until years later when my mother told me who my daddy was and how it came to be. She hated him and she hated me. But we went to church every time those doors were open so she could flaunt his illegitimate daughter in front of his face."

"So that's why this case was so important to you. It hit home." He nodded his head in understanding.

"Yes. It hit hard. It brought back ugly memories I have fought hard to make go away. That's why I do what I do today. It's why I am who I am. I was going to prove to all of them I had value. They were going to see I could make something of my life without them. I was tough enough to stand alone." As she said it he watched her posture herself by sitting straighter and raising her chin just so.

"You don't have to prove anything to me. I know you have value. I promise I won't try to take anything away from you. I just want to be your friend."

"Teo, why? Why do you think you want to be my friend?" She was asking the question honestly. Her posture soften just a little.

His answer surprised even him, "I like you. I'd like to spend sometime finding out who you are. You

170

interest me. I'd like to sit and talk. Take long walks. Maybe even hold your hand."

Her look was quiet and pensive; then she said, "Okay. Walks. Maybe hands. No church. Not yet."

"That will do for a start."

She finished half of her sandwich. Neatly folded the other half back into the wrap; handed him her pickle and said, "Thanks for lunch. Let's see what your client's letters looks like, then I'll decide what to do next." Standing she headed towards her car. A few steps down the walk she turned back, smiled and said, "I'll look forward to your call."

She started to turn when he called out, "Hey...Did they ever appreciate the value in you?"

She paused just for a moment then answered, "He developed Alzheimer's and died not knowing anyone or anything. My mom seems quite proud of me; I send her money monthly." She turned and walked away.

Teo watched as she got in her car and drove away. He said out loud, *Wow! What have I gotten myself into this time? That is a lot of hurt bundled in one woman.*

Even so, he found himself chuckling as he walked back to his office. *This should be interesting if it's anything.*

Chapter Eleven

Psalm 32:11

Rejoice in the LORD

and be glad,

you righteous;

Sing, all you who are

upright in heart!

THE FOURTH OF JULY DAWNED WITH THE PROMISE of a beautiful day. The temperature was already rising and the plan was to go to the park for the day. There would be beautiful fireworks at dark. It would be a walk through memory lane. This was the same park where Brad had proposed to Noelle and she was anxious to be back there again.

The moms, as usual, had been cooking all morning, while Noelle, feeling a little lazy, slept in. The last few days she had begun to feel the uncomfortable pressure on her back that signified to her the weight of her belly was pulling on her spine. Brad had been giving her back rubs at night to relieve the pressure. However, her only relief came as she would lower herself into a warm tub of water and soak the pains away.

He would question her, "Are you sure that you're feeling okay? Maybe you should stop going to the restaurant and just rest more? After all in a few weeks, your hands are going to be full and your life will never be your own again. Maybe we should call the doctor's office just to be on the safe side?"

"Silly...I love it that you're concerned for me. I'm fine. My back just isn't used to carrying all of this weight in front. Pregnancy is a natural process not a disease. Remember? She would laugh as she asked, "How many back rubs do you give to your mommy cows?"

He noticed she wasn't sleeping well at night. With her up and down all night long, he wasn't either.

"What do you expect?" She would say. "Every time this little one moves, I have to go to the bathroom.

Besides we better get ready to be up through the night, at least for a while. I hear that's their favorite time to play with their daddy."

"You hear that huh? Well...I hear they only want their mommy when it's middle of the night and they're crying. It isn't like I can let her suckle on a nipple. I don't come with those parts."

The teasing continued every day as they became more and more comfortable with each other and more and more excited about the new baby about to join their family.

This morning though, Noelle pulled herself from the cozy bed and went into the bathroom. Choosing a warm tub soak instead of a quick shower, she hoped the relaxing water would calm the tight muscles that were nagging her back continually. Today she wanted to be able to enjoy every minute of their time at the park. She wanted to spend the day with the man she loved; walking back to the bench where he had asked her to marry him. It would be a perfect day; a day that was all about them.

Brad came to see if she was going to stay in bed all day. He was surprised to find her fast asleep in the tub. A sight that made him think of other things than playing at the park. He loved the smell of her and the little girl look as she lay there covered with only her head and toes sticking out from the bubbles. Leaning over he kissed her cheek. As she slowly opened her eyes, reality set in and she remembered she was in the tub.

"How long have I been in here?" She asked stretching.

Brad felt the water. "Long enough for the water to get cold. You better get out."

"No...I think I should drain this tub of water and fill it again. It feels so good on my back."

174

"Are you sure you're up to this day at the Park?"

"Absolutely. This day you are going to push me in the swing; take me for a walk to our bench; feed me wonderful food; you know...Dote on me!" She laughed.

"Really. The 'dote on me part' isn't any different than any other day. I love to dote on you." Brad said as he pulled the plug on the tub and turned the water on to warm again. When the water was ready, he plugged the tub back up and let the water fill to almost overflowing.

On his way out the door he said, "It's a good thing we don't have city water. You would cost me a fortune."

Noelle soaked for a while longer, washed her hair under the shower and got dressed. All the time thinking she just wanted to get back into the water where her back felt so much better. Tonight. She would soak again after they returned from the park. For now she just wouldn't think about the wonderful relief that came with the water in the tub. As she bounded down the stairs, she decided she would think about their adventures for the day.

"Brad...I'm ready!"

****

Eyan was home and planning on a full day with the families. He was looking forward to being together. His contribution on the day was an early arrival at the park so they got the same tables they had when they were there in the fall. The boys were kept busy by the girls who needed their swings pushed higher and higher. Nissa and Anaya spent a big part of the day swimming with Eyan. The water was warm and the air was perfect. They couldn't have asked for a better day.

Brad and Noelle strolled knee deep in the sandy entrance of the lake. Noelle just wasn't comfortable

175

getting into the water. She was concerned about bacteria that could be in there. She was too close to delivery to want to take any chances. However, she loved the sun on her as she walked through the waves holding hands with the man she loved.

Genie and Angelina relaxed in the sun watching their families play.

Mid afternoon, Brad and Noelle had snuck off for their walk down the trail. They had found their bench and Brad had gotten down on one knee again and asked, "Will you continue to be my wife for the rest of my life?"

"Yes." Noelle answered, "Forever and ever."

Hearing those words, Brad reached into his pocket and pulled out a velvet box and handed it to Noelle.

Surprised, Noelle looked at him.

"Go ahead. Open it up."

Slowly she opened the box and gasped at what she saw. A beautiful mother and child necklace with a July birthstone inside.

"It's beautiful. Brad, thank you."

"Now this is assuming that you are going to pop that baby out yet this month. If I'm wrong, we'll change the stone." He took the necklace from its box and fastened it around her neck saying, "You are beautiful."

"I should have a gift for you. You are always giving me presents." She pretended to pout.

"My gift comes with two arms, two legs and ten fingers and toes. You're about to give me the most precious gift of all. Have I told you lately that I can't wait."

"Only every day." She laughed.

He could only shrug and confess, "Guilty!"

"Come on, let's walk some more." She said. The

176

reality was she just couldn't sit any longer. As much as she was enjoying the day, her back was really getting uncomfortable and that bath tub was sounding more and more promising.

By the end of the fireworks, Noelle was as uncomfortable as she could ever remember being. She was up and down. Standing, swaying and pacing.

Genie and Angelina were keeping a close eye on her. "Honey are you sure you don't want to go home?" Her mother asked.

"No." She snapped. "I'm sorry. I just can't find a comfortable position. There's just so much baby packed in here." She said rubbing her tummy. "It pulls so hard on my back."

Genie had noticed the baby had dropped quite low in the last couple of weeks. She surmised to say that was a good thing. The more of the labor process that would happen before hand, the easier time Noelle would have on the actual birth day. Still she wished it didn't have to be so hard for her daughter. Having gone through birth three times, she knew how uncomfortable you could be in that last month.

Brad pulled Noelle down onto his lap and began to rub in circular motions across her back.

"Have I ever told you how much I love those magical hands." She whispered so only the two of them could hear.

"Tell me more." He whispered back into her ear.

"I love what you do with those hands. They make everything better." She said.

He laughed, "The cows feel the same way."

Noelle lovingly smacked his leg.

"Make sure they know you belong to someone else. I won't share."

177

"Don't worry your pretty head. You are married to a one woman farmer." Brad continued the silly talk trying to keep her mind off of her back.

As the fireworks ended, Brad and Noelle were the first ones out of the park. In fact they had left a little early trying to beat the rush. They had seen the finale over the lake as they were driving down the road.

They "Oooohed" and "Aaaaahed" as they made their way back to the farm.

Before Brad could unload the truck, he heard the water running in the tub. He was beginning to wonder about this pain in her back. Tomorrow he would call the doctor's office even if Noelle refused.

Brad found Noelle up to her neck in warm water again, sleeping away when he finished downstairs. He thought to himself, *If this baby doesn't come soon, I'm going to be married to a prune.* Worried about her drowning, he sat on the stool and just watched her sleep. It wasn't a chore. He loved to just watch her breathe. He sat there and prayed for her and the baby; for the rest of their family and for their life together.

Father, as we get closer to the time this baby is going to enter the world, I ask You send Your angels to surround Noelle and Baby Girl. I'm asking for an easy delivery for both mommy and baby. We rest in Your ever present care. We love You and we trust You. Amen.

Noelle woke up and saw Brad sitting on the stool by the tub. "Are you watching me sleep again?"

"Someone has to be ready to save you when you go under. You know, you really have got to stop sleeping in the tub with all of that water. Without my quick and agile moves...Well it could be ugly."

"You're silly." She said as she struggled to get out of the tub.

178

"Let me help you." He said as he cautiously helped her stand up. "I watched you lay there with just the top of your belly out of the water, you know what I thought about?"

She hesitated to ask knowing it couldn't be good. "What?"

"Easter eggs. Dying Easter eggs. You know how you put them into the cup and the top always sticks up...

"Ohhhh..." She grabbed the towel and started snapping it at him. "That is a terrible thing to say to a pregnant woman."

"Hey...Hey...Hey!" He grabbed her and held her tight. "You are the most beautiful woman ever. Pregnant or not." She began to calm as he kissed her slowly and thoroughly.

"Here slip this over your head and climb into the bed. I'll take a quick shower...If you've left me any hot water. Then I'll massage your back pain away."

Doing as he said, Noelle got under the sheet and waited as Brad got ready for bed.

Coming from the bathroom, Brad saw Noelle was sound asleep. Not wanting to disturb her, he carefully turned off the light and eased himself under the sheets.

It was only a few hours later when Brad woke to Noelle's moaning in her sleep. He listened as she quieted and then was almost back to sleep when she started moaning again. Thinking about the day she had, he began to wonder, *Could she be in labor? The pain in her back, could it be back labor?*

Rolling over he grabbed his watch off the bedside table and waited. Sure enough the moaning was happening for about a minute. There were three minutes in between episodes. Reality was setting in. Three minutes...That can't be good.

Brad wrapped his arms around Noelle just as she started to moan again. "Honey...Noelle...Wake up!"

She did with a start, "What? Oh my back is hurting so much."

"Noelle, I think you're in labor. You've been moaning and I've been timing it. It's happening every three minutes. The moans are about a minute long."

"I can't be in labor. I just need to get in the tub."

"No more tub." We're going to the hospital."

"I can't. I don't want to move. I'm going to the bathroom."

Getting out of bed took a lot of effort for Noelle. She had just walked into the bathroom when she let out a small scream. Brad came running. She held up her hand signalling him to stop.

"Don't. It's all wet. My water just broke."

Having said that, she grabbed her back and stretched backwards. "Ohhhhh my gosh!"

Brad was by her side holding her and rubbing her back as he was thinking, *We're going to have a baby.* He couldn't just stand here with her. He was going to have to call an ambulance. He helped her sit on the toilet and said, "Don't go anywhere and don't drop that baby into the toilet. I'll be right back."

"Don't leave me."

"Listen to me. We have to be calm. I'm going to call an ambulance. I think we're going to have a baby soon. I'm going to get Mom to help me. I'll just be a minute. Okay?" He kissed her forehead.

"Okay. Hurry." She answered grabbing her back and stretching, "Hurry. Please."

Brad ran part way down the stairs and yelled, "Mom. Eyan. Come quick."

Instantly the two of them, sleepy eyed, were

running up the stairs. "What's the matter?"

"I think we're about to have a baby. I think Noelle has been in labor all day and we didn't know it. Eyan call 911 and then boil some water. Mom will you put some kind of protective barrier on the bed. Get me towels. Lots of towels. Hurry." He turned and ran back into the bedroom.

Grabbing their bath towels, he mopped up the water on the bathroom floor. His mom was in the bedroom throwing an extra shower curtain over the sheets and then putting another fitted sheet on top of that.

"Okay." Angelina said calmly. "Do you need help getting Noelle back here?"

Brad, stroking her hair asked, "Honey can you walk back to the bed?"

"Aren't we going to the hospital?"

I'm afraid we're past that point. Eyan has called 911. Better the ambulance come to us now." Brad seemed calm and sure.

"What about the baby?" Brad could hear the panic in Noelle's voice.

"Baby Girl is going to be fine. She's just going to be an early bird. I've done this hundreds of times. I'm a pro."

"Brad...**I'm not a cow!**" Noelle yelled.

Taking her face gently into his hands, "Do you trust me Noelle?"

Without hesitation she answered, "Yes", as the tears trickled down her cheeks.

"Okay. Listen to me. I will protect you and the baby with everything inside of me. Come with me to the bed and let me get you comfortable. God is with us. Everything is going to be all right."

"Are you sure?"

"Listen, if a barn was safe enough for His son to come into this world, then our bedroom is even better. Are you with me?"

"Okay." She answered as another pain gripped her back.

"Mom...Stack those pillows up and sit up against them. I'm going to have you hold Noelle up against you."

"Brad?" Noelle half screamed as another pain grabbed her again.

Wrapping his arms around her, he took his fist and began pressure in circular motions on the low of her back. He whispered in her ear. "Breathe with me." He began to imitate quick breaths in and out. A nice rhythmic pant. She followed his lead.

When the contraction was past he helped position her onto the bed with her knees up on pillows.

"I'm going to do a quick check and see what we have going on. Okay?"

Noelle nodded her head as she began to pant again. Angelina was putting pressure on Noelle's lower back.

There was a knock on the door and Eyan said, "The ambulance is on the way. I called Noelle's mom. They're coming too. I've got hot water out here."

Brad winked at Noelle and slipped off the end of the bed. Going to the door he took the water and peroxide from his brother.

"Are we okay?" Eyan asked.

"Yup...We're fine. We're going to have a baby."

"I'll start praying. You got this one big brother."

"Prayer is good."

Brad went back into the room and set the water tub down on the stand. Inside the hot water was a pair of scissors, a kitchen clamp and a nose suction bulb. "Thanks Eyan." He said as he took the items out and laid them on a towel. Then he started scrubbing up his arms. He took one of the towels and placed it under Noelle's bottom.

"Brad, I'm scared."

"Noelle, listen to me. You are not scared. God is in control. Everything is going just as it should. With your contractions, the baby's head is crowning. It won't be very long and we're going to hold our baby. We're good! Everything is good! Okay?"

"Okay." She answered timidly.

Brad watched through a couple more contractions all the time asking God to let him know when it was time. After the fourth contraction, he knew God was saying go.

"Okay Baby. This time is it. When I tell you to push, you push with everything in you and don't stop until I say stop. Ready...PUSH!"

Noelle took a deep breath and held it as she pushed and pushed and pushed with Brad coaching her the whole way.

"Keep pushing. Come on Noelle. You're doing a great job. Don't stop. PUSH. PUSH. PUSH."

"Okay. Okay. Stop pushing and breathe. Come on. Breathe. I have a head. On the next contraction we're going to do it all again and once I get these shoulder out, I bet we're going to have a baby. Deep breaths.

"I don't know when I'm having a contraction." Noelle cried out.

"Don't worry. I'm going to tell you when to push. Take a deep breath again. Ready? One. Two. Three." He was watching her body respond waiting for the contraction. "Okay here we go. Deep breath...And

183

here we go. One more time Noelle. Give me a PUSH...
PUSH...PUSH...PUSH...PUSH...PUSH...PUSH...
PUSH...And STOP!"

Instantly, in one quick move, Noelle felt the pressure on her back leave. Noelle's eyes were closed while she was pushing. She heard Brad laughing. Opening her eyes she took a picture that will stay with her forever. There was Brad on his knees holding their baby. The baby was kicking and flailing. Brad jumped off the bed and grabbed the suction bulb. He began to suction nose and mouth. Then the sweetest sound she had ever heard, the baby was crying. Nothing weak about those lungs. Screams of anger belted out of that little body.

The tears were flowing down as she said, "What is it?"

"Seriously you have to ask? It's a girl." Brad was laughing as the tears were running down his face.

Noelle was laughing and crying all at the same time, "Of course she is. Why would I doubt?"

Brad laid the baby in Noelle's arms. "Hold her tight Momma. We're going to have a few more contractions and then we'll be all done."

Noelle could feel her body start to finish the process of birth. Following the instructions that Brad gave her she pushed a couple more times and they were done.

"Great job. Beautiful. You're a pro." Brad encouraged his wife as he finished.

Brad yelled for Eyan to get him a large ziplock bag so he could prepare for the hospital. He wanted to make sure he had done everything correctly. He wanted the doctor to check everything over and make sure Noelle was safe from infection. Washing up his hands, he went to check out his beautiful new daughter.

Noelle was in awe of the precious bundle with huge eyes staring straight into her face. She was perfect. Baby Girl began to nuzzle.

Angelina, who was still holding Noelle, said through tears, "She wants to nurse."

"Will you help us, please?"

Angelina helped mommy and baby get settled. Baby Girl knew just what she wanted and the transition was as smooth as silk.

There was a knock on the door and Noelle heard her mother's voice.

Brad threw a sheet over Noelle and went to answer the door.

"Come in and meet your granddaughter and niece." He said to Genie and the girls.

Genie gave him a quick hug and then stood looking at the most precious sight. Her daughter was snuggling with her baby at her breast.

Brad heard the sirens signalling the arrival of the ambulance.

Eyan brought them up the stairs and to the room where everyone was now ooohing and aaahing over the little bundle that had just entered their lives.

"Looks like everything is under control here. You don't even need us." The Medic stated.

"We need a ride. We're going to the hospital to get checked out. Just to be sure." Brad announced.

Angelina suggested, "Why don't you all go to the hospital. I'll just tidy up the room while you're gone."

"No. I'll stay and help you." Genie offered.

"Absolutely not. You go with your daughter. It won't take me long. Then I'll come down too." Angelina insisted.

"Thanks Mom." Brad kissed her on the cheek.

"No Son. Thank you. You just brought a miracle into the world and I'm so proud of you." Angelina kissed him one more time. "Take care of my granddaughter. Oh? Does she have a name?"

"Yes. Yes. What's her name?" Nissa and Anaya both squealed with anticipation.

Noelle held her forward and said, "Let me introduce you to Emma Rae Conroy. Emma means 'one who is complete'. She completes us as a family."

"Ohhhh! Perfect! We love it!" The name was received well by all.

On the way out the door Brad saw Eyan. "Thanks Brother! I couldn't have done it without you. Great prayer. Worked perfect."

"You did good. She's beautiful. Next time let's try the hospital though. Little nervous here. I just got to say."

The brothers hugged and slapped each others' backs; then Brad headed out to the ambulance.

$$* * * * * * * * * * * * * * * *$$

In the quiet of the hospital room after everyone had gone home, Brad lay beside Noelle as the two of them snuggled their beautiful sleeping prize.

Noelle began to cry.

"What's wrong Honey."

"She's so beautiful and perfect. What if I hadn't found you. What if..."

"Shshshshshsh. Don't ever think it again. That's how big our God is. He has great works planned for our daughter. There's a purpose for her life. He'll use us to protect other babies. We can now speak to other mothers who think they don't have any options. We'll just ask

God to open doors for us so we can be used by Him. He'll show us just how 'BIG' He is."

"Mr. Bradley Conroy can I just tell you one more time how special you are and how blessed I am to have you as my husband. What a great job you did today." Noelle beamed at the man of her dreams.

"Are you serious? You did the most work. You were amazing."

"I couldn't have done any of this without you." Noelle leaned her head against the shoulder that represented strength to her.

"All in a days work Mrs. Conroy. All in a days work."

Epilogue

A QUICK NIGHT STAY WITH A PRONOUNCEMENT OF health for both mommy and baby was enough for both Brad and Noelle. They were eager to get home and begin their life with their new bundle of joy.

Both families were waiting for them when they arrived. Eyan had driven to the hospital that morning to bring them home. He had a hidden agenda. He wanted some alone time with his new little niece. He knew once they got home, he would have to battle all of the women for baby time. Eyan was smart enough to know he would lose. So he, very unselfishly, volunteered his time to run to the hospital. He went early and once there he was in no hurry to leave.

Brad watched as his brother gingerly cuddled and cooed sweet sounds to the little one in his arms.

"Looks pretty natural for you Bro."

"Feels pretty good too. She's amazing. You can just see God's hand at work on every part of her." Taking his man sized hands and gingerly tracing every little fold of her ear he marveled, "Look at those tiny little ears. And her lips are perfectly shaped." Placing his finger into her little fist he said, "Just look at her fingers with those perfectly pink finger nails. I bet her toes look the same way." Eyan just shook his head. "I never knew I could love someone this much and she isn't even mine. You must be bursting inside."

"I can't even put it into words. I didn't even sleep last night. I couldn't take my eyes off her or her mother. They're both more than I even hoped for." Brad then rubbed his eyes to wipe away the moisture.

"I get it. I really do." Eyan nodded; himself feeling a little teary.

"What do you get?" Noelle asked as she came from behind the bathroom door towel drying her hair.

"How lucky you guys are; and how awesome God is."

Noelle sat down on the bed beside her husband. "I get it too." She smiled as Brad wrapped his arms around her and kissed her forehead.

Eyan handed his new little niece back to her father and shook his head, "I can't believe I'm about to say this, but I guess we should go. There's a house full of people waiting back there to snatch this new arrival right out of our hands. If we don't get a move on it, they're all going to be headed this way."

Laughing Brad began to gather everything together while Noelle paged the nurse saying they were ready to leave. Noelle sat down in the wheelchair that had been dropped off earlier with strict orders that baby and mommy were to ride to the car in the luxury ride. That was where they were found by transport when they came to usher them out to start their new life together as a family.

****

Arriving back at the farm, they were greeted with balloons and flowers welcoming home baby Emma. The grandmas and aunts were more than willing to take the bundle from the tired parents' arms.

"Get in line Bro." Brad said to Eyan as Noelle handed off the baby.

Eyan whispered into his Brother's ear, "Why do you think I volunteered to go to the hospital. Baby time!"

"Smart."

Nothing short of the wonderful lunch would have been expected from Angelina. Afterwards mommy and baby settled down for a little nap.

As they shared the quiet of the bedroom, a soft tap was heard along with a whispered, "Knock...knock."

"Come in." Brad said as Genie opened the door.

"We forgot. This letter and these flowers both came for you before you got home." Genie apologized.

Noelle opened the card on the flowers and began to read.

To my precious daughter and her new family. I remember the day well when I brought you home. I couldn't have been more proud. I hope this beautiful little girl brings you as much joy as you brought me. Love Dad.

Noelle looked at Genie, who had lost all color, and asked, "How did he know?"

"I don't know. This fast. I don't know!" Genie answered.

Brad had been sitting in the chair watching the emotions play out as they read the card. He wondered too...Less than 24 hours? Something didn't seem right about that. It left him feeling a little eerie.

While he was thinking about it, he opened the letter that had come to the house. Skimming over it he immediately wondered if this was a good thing for Noelle right now.

"What is that?" She asked.

"Ummmm." He wasn't sure how to answer.

She looked at him with a peculiar look on her

face. It wasn't like him to hide things from her. "Brad? What is it?"

"Maybe later," he answered.

"You can't do that. Now I have to know."

"It's a letter from Delmyn Whitehall."

The thought took her breath away. Why would he send her a letter? Immediately fear came over her as she looked at the baby sleeping so peacefully in the cradle by her bed.

Protectively pulling Emma closer she asked again with fear, "Brad?"

Brad quickly read through the letter and then answered, "It's okay. Do you want me to read it to you?"

Genie sat down on the bed beside her daughter and took her hand.

"Go ahead." Noelle answered.

To The Person I Hurt:

I know this must come as a surprise to hear from me. I want to assure you that I mean no harm. I have already caused you more anguish than any person should cause another.

I am writing to say how very sorry I am for all I did. I hope someday you will find it in your heart to forgive me. What I did was inexcusable. I deserve the sentence I will be serving. I just hope the God I have found will heal all of the brokenness that I have caused.

I know you are pregnant. There are not words to tell you how much I wish I had been a better person. I wish I hadn't hurt you. I have asked God to be my Savior and to forgive my sins. I hope someday you will be able to forgive me also.

192

I know you have talked with my parents. They told me what you said. I agree with your decisions. Please don't tell the baby about me ever. I wouldn't want the baby to associate itself with such a hideous act. I don't want to be responsible for messing up one more life.

I pray that out of this ugliness may come some kind of blessing for you and for the baby.

Again, I know I don't deserve it; but I hope that someday you will be able to forgive me and put the past behind you. I truly am sorry for all of the pain I inflicted onto your life.

Sincerely,
Delmyn Whitehall

Thoughts From The Author

I HOPE ALL OF YOU HAVE ENJOYED THE TIME YOU'VE spent journeying with Noelle, Brad and their families. You've been a part of their history as they've begun a walk that will continue through at least one more book.

In the first book, **SAVING NOELLE,** we learned of God's love for us. We discovered His willingness to chase us no matter how far we run. God never wants His children living in their darkest hour. His Word, The Bible, tells us He is the lamp that will light our way. He doesn't want us to stumble and fall. However, if we do, He's there to pick us up and carry us if He must. Noelle ran, not knowing who He was. In her running, God made a way for her to find Him. You see, He'll never leave us out there by ourselves. We can only be separated from Him by our choice, not by His.

God gave others the opportunity to receive blessings he had waiting for them, when He opened the doors for them to help Noelle and they walked through. Angelina was willing to share the saddest time of her life. Through that willingness to be obedient, even when it hurt, Noelle was able to find her way to a loving Savior. By finding Him, she was able to make the right decisions when it came to the life of her baby. God opened His arms wide and Noelle came, broken and spilled out, willing to be captured by His love.

As we moved into the second book in the **Carried By Angels Series , PERFECT LOVE,** we see how God is masterminding Noelle's healing and giving her a future. The Lord gave us His promise through the prophet Jeremiah, *"For I know the plans I have for you," declares the LORD, "Plans to prosper you and not to harm you, plans to give you hope and a future. Then you will call upon me and come and pray to me, and I will listen to you. You will seek Me and find Me when you seek Me with all your heart. I will be found by you," declares the LORD, "and will bring you back from captivity. Jeremiah 29:11.* It was Brad's plan to make sure he was waiting on the Lord and because of his obedience, we watched as God gave him a future. God used Noelle, broken and desperate, to fulfill the desires of Brad's heart. God used Brad to open the door to an amazing new life in the Lord for Noelle.

I marvel at how God works. Let's look at the Prophet Elijah. He showed unconditional loyalty to the Lord and God took care of him. Elijah called forth a drought in the land to punish the nation for it's idolatry. Yet God had him go to a place of peace where he could drink and God sent ravens to feed him. Then when the brook dried up because of the drought, God sent him to a widow who was going to eat her last meal with her son and then die for lack of food. Elijah told her, under the direction of the Lord, to feed him first. She obeyed and made that last meal for Elijah and the Lord made her "meals plenty". See how God used someone who was desperate to minister to Elijah. God gave the widow a chance to be obedient; which then allowed God to bless the widow and her son. You can find this story in I Kings 17:1-16.

Brad and Angelina were blessed because they were willing to be obedient. Noelle was blessed because, even in her darkest hour, she surrendered all to the Lord.

In the third book, **FORGIVING FREEDOM**,

we watched as the opportunity for forgiveness tore open healed wounds. Just like faith is a verb, so is forgiving. It requires an action that isn't always comfortable. Brad and Noelle, with a bright new future looming ahead of them, were willing to walk into the darkness to see true freedom abound.

Out of that walk God continued to open up new doors for them to serve using what He had given them.

As always, it's been my pleasure to open up another page in the life of the characters we have come to love. I hope, as God writes their story for you, we'll see them rise up to the occasion God had created for them. My prayer will be that God's principles will be lived out on the pages of their story books. I pray you will be able to find Him in the midst of the words.

I hope you'll be pleasantly surprised to find that once again, the Lord has continued their message of love, hope and mercy into yet another book. Wait as **REDEEMING GRACE** will bring us to the final chapters of Noelle's journey into a life filled with God and His mysteries. As is usual for me, I only write when God says write and it was just recently He dropped this fourth book in the **Carried By Angels Series** into my spirit. I'm excited to start writing and see how God is going to bring closure to what has been an emotional journey for and so many of you. Thank you for your words of encouragement and love and for your willingness to share your stories of brokenness...And yes, courage. I have treasured the opportunities I've had to discuss with you the walks that so many of you have had through the pains and sufferings of abortions. I pray each of you will be able to find the God who forgives and embrace true healing in His arms.

As always, if you have not ever accepted Jesus

as your Lord and Savior, I would count it a pleasure to be able to walk through that prayer with you. It is that simple. Jesus came so you could have life and have it more abundantly. He wants to spend eternity with you. He willingly went to the cross for that very purpose. If there had only been you on this earth, He would still have willingly laid down His life on that tree just for you. Now is the perfect time. Just repeat after me this simple prayer of love for a God who gave it all for you.

Lord Jesus, I come to You completely surrendered. I realize I need a Savior. I confess I am a sinner and that I need You. I want to be Your child and heir to Your eternal kingdom. I believe You died on the cross for my sins. I believe You were dead and buried and that on the third day You rose from the grave. Thank you for cleansing me from my sins; for removing them as far as the east is from the west. I am grateful You see me white as snow. Thank you for making me a new creation. My old ways are gone and now I am a new creature bought and paid for by the precious blood of Jesus. I am now Your child never to be separated from You again. By praying this prayer I have sealed my place in Heaven forever to live with You. I acknowledge I could never be worthy without You and only by Your grace can I be free. Thank You for forgiving me and for loving me as Your own. In Jesus Name. Amen.

My hope is you prayed with me and the heavens are rejoicing right now. If so, congratulations! Now take the next step. Get a Bible and begin to read His words. They are life changing.

God bless you and yours. May all of your dreams come true as you encounter the "Living Lord".

God loves you...Be CAPTURED!

BRENDA

Angel Wing Ministries

"Come to me, all you who are weary and burdened, and I will give You rest. Take my yoke upon you and learn from me, for I am gentle and humble in heart, and you will find rest for your souls. For my yoke is easy and my burden is light.
Matthew 11:28-30

While we were yet sinners, Christ died for us.
Romans 5:8

For I know the plans I have for you, declares the Lord, plans to prosper you and not to harm you, plans to give you hope and a future.
Jeremiah 29:11

Therefore, if anyone is in Christ, he is a new creation; the old is gone, the new has come.
II Corinthians 5:17

These books continue to be an obedience to serve God. It is still my desire that whoever reads these words will find a burning passion to know my savior more.

I would love to hear from you.

Communicate with us on

**Facebook
At
Angel Wing Ministries**

or

bconley9446@yahoo.com

We are also working on a web page at
www.angelwingministries.com

We are a work in progress!

Watch for book four of the...

Carried By Angels Series

REDEEMING GRACE

Coming Soon

REDEEMING GRACE

I CORINTHIANS 13:1-13

1. If I speak in the tongues of men and of angels, but have not love, I am only a resounding gong or a clanging cymbal.

Michael Dunn hurried through the hallways that would quickly lead him to the room of his Great Aunt Denise. *Why am I here?* He wondered to himself for an uncountable time today. He had made a promise to his mother earlier in the week he would stop in and say a quick hello. That is why he had driven so far out of his way. Truth be known, his mother had made him feel guilty. He couldn't even talk any of his family into going with him. Running through his mind were all of the reasons why they couldn't come. Everyone of them finding excuses because of their busy lives. Well, who did they think they were talking to. As Dean of Students at the University, his schedule was already so full he hadn't really wanted to add this one more stop. He didn't really have time for any of this. Especially when you considered this trip would cost him a good three hours out of his day.

Thinking about that time frame made him walk even faster through the halls that smelled so much like bleach and old people. In all honesty, if it wasn't for his mother's pleading, he would never come here. The smells always made him think of how life leads to the unavoidable. After all, it is appointed unto every man to die. Those smells hit him the minute he walked in through the door. He referred to them as the smells of death. Bleach and old. You know the smells that remind you life slips away before you know it. The same smells stay with you long after you have walked away from a facility like this, even while patting yourself on the back for doing the right thing when it wasn't what you want to do. He wasn't even sure if the smell was real or just a figment of his own imagination. This is why he hated the smell of disinfectant. To Michael Dunn it was just a reminder of his own mortality.

After all, isn't that why people came to places like this? Didn't they come to die? He never saw them coming here to live. They called it assisted living; but Michael thought there had to be a better way to end your life than lying in a bed waiting for someone to come for a visit. He pictured himself lying their waiting until he visually saw himself take his last breath on this earth. Then the guilt crept in. It could be him someday and he would certainly want someone to come for a visit; just for a few moments of reprieve in what had to be a completely tedious existence.

Okay Michael. You've made the drive this far. Stop complaining to yourself and make the most of this. You are about to brighten your aunt's day. Consider this your good deed and do it with a smile on your face.

Plus, it would appease his mother who, even though he was 58 years old, could take him back to those moments of childhood. Just the tone of her voice as she scolded, "Michael". Even though she didn't say it, he could finish her sentence with "Really"? Instantly he returned to those years before he grew up and into success. There he was in the years of plaid shorts, white dress shirts topped off with the perfectly tied clip on black tie. Not to mention the waxed hair laying so closely to his head that air could not possibly circulate through it. He almost chuckled thinking back on those early pictures. There he would be so stiff; almost as stiff as his hair. He wondered why no one but his mother and sisters were smiling. Along with him, his father and brothers all had the same look. They all seemed so somber you could almost hear the words as they were raging through their heads. *Are we done yet?* Although not a one of them would have dared utter that sentence.

Even as his steps carried him closer to his aunt, he could hear his mother's voice. "Just how long has it been since you have taken time to visit your Great Aunt Denise. You know you were always her favorite and she never missed your parties or special events. She always brought you that one particular gift you had been waiting for all year. Honestly Michael, we don't know how much longer she is going to be with us and you owe her an occasional visit in her last days."

He knew better than to argue. She was always ready to prove she was right about this matter. In his heart of hearts, he knew she was.

So here he was walking as quickly as he could through the hallway that brought him to the nurses' station. Michael hesitated before deciding to turn left. It had been sometime since he had been here and if memory served him correctly, he should make a sharp turn here. Pretty sure he had made the correct move, he made quick peeks into the rooms he passed. He didn't remember her being in a hall with so many men. He began to question if he had gone the right way just as he reached the suite

204

at the end of the hall. His aunt had been in this room for all the years he had been coming to visit her; however, this didn't look quite right to him.

He read the sign beside the door and it said, "Mr. Smith". Obviously, that was not his aunt.

Michael started to turn around just as a sight inside of the door caught his attention. A sitting room separated the hallway from the actual living area. There was a second door opening into that room. Inside that second room was a man lying in the bed all the way over by the window. Something familiar jumped in his spirit, a moment that gave him pause and in an instant he knew why. The man lying so very still in that bed was someone he knew, someone he loved. He wanted to run before he saw any more; but it felt as if his feet were glued to the spot where he was standing. He had to be wrong. It couldn't be true. What he was looking at had to be a mistake. It wasn't possible.

His mind began to scream, *Get out...Before he sees you...Get out.* He stood for only a few more seconds; though the time felt like it was ticking away ever so quickly. Then he turned and ran. Michael ran down the hall and out of the hallway that should have taken him to his great aunt's room. Instead it took him into a moment in time he could never forget. He had stepped into a nightmare of sorts. Just what the story was, he wasn't sure. What he did know was he had to get out of there before he was sick. He could feel the bile rising up into his throat as he almost ran down the halls and back out into the entryway that had started his journey into the black hole of reality. Bursting through the outside doors, he could feel himself gasping for air as if the trip back into the outside world had squeezed his chest so hard he couldn't breathe. Try as he may, he could not expel the sound that signaled a continued motion of voluntary effort made by his lungs. Then it came. More violent than seemed possible, his stomach emptied its contents behind a nearby bush. Standing with his hand on the cold brick of the building as it held him in space, it came over and over and over again, and then the end.

Forcing himself to pull air in through his nose and exhale it slowly through his mouth several times, Michael found the center of his universe. In those moments of repeating a very normal pattern of taking air in and blowing air out, he calmed himself enough to realize he needed to get to a safe place. Heading to his parked car, he quickly grabbed the keys out of his suit pants and clicked the button that unlocked the door. Climbing into the drivers seat and lying his head against the cool of the steering wheel leather, Michael began to try to convince himself what he had just witnessed was not true. Yet, in his heart of hearts, and confirmed by his own eyes, he knew it was true.

What did it all mean? He knew what he had just seen. What he didn't know was how did he explain that actual moment of vision. It couldn't be true. Maybe his eyes had played a horrible trick on him? But no...He knew...He just knew. He had seen it and the picture was playing over and over in his mind. With every frame, he was drawn further and further into the reality of what he had just witnessed. What he didn't know was what he was going to do with it. Realizing he needed sometime to process that picture of truth, Michael sat until the shaking of his hands subsided and he knew he would be safe to make the drive back into the city that held comfort and familiarity for him. He needed the noise of the traffic and the bumper to bumper chaos that comes with rush hour. His plans had changed and now he needed time to find that one perfect word that would right his world again. He had to find something that would put his center back where it was supposed to be, spinning perfectly on point. He needed peace.

PROVERBS 16:3
Commit to the Lord whatever you do; And your plans will succeed.

God Bless You

Notes

<u>Notes</u>

<u>Notes</u>

Carried By Angels Series

BOOK ONE
SAVING NOELLE

BOOK TWO
PERFECT LOVE

BOOK THREE
FORGIVING FREEDOM

BOOK FOUR
REDEEMING GRACE